For Camille

Cheers, Steve

Please enjoy!

Woman
BEHIND
HOME PLATE

J. STEPHEN THOMPSON

 FriesenPress

One Printers Way
Altona, MB R0G 0B0
Canada

www.friesenpress.com

Copyright © 2023 by J. Stephen Thompson
First Edition — 2023

All rights reserved.

No part of this publication may be reproduced in any form, or by any means, electronic or mechanical, including photocopying, recording, or any information browsing, storage, or retrieval system, without permission in writing from FriesenPress.

ISBN
978-1-03-917573-0 (Hardcover)
978-1-03-917572-3 (Paperback)
978-1-03-917574-7 (eBook)

1. FICTION, LITERARY

Distributed to the trade by The Ingram Book Company

This book is entirely a work of fiction. While reference may be made to actual events or existing locations, the names, characters, places, and incidents are either the product of the author's imagination or are used fictitiously. Any resemblance to any actual persons, living or dead, business establishments, team names, events or locales is entirely coincidental. When places or names are identified, it is only for geographic and historical accuracy. Every effort has been made to ensure the accuracy of historical events.

Acknowledgements

I wish to thank many for their contributions to the otherwise solitary exercise of writing, especially my friends and family who read all or part of one or more versions of the manuscript and/or listened to sections read aloud: Fred and Trudy, Merv and Andrea, Alex and Catherine, Susan, Bob, Annemieke, Linda, Jane, the Troupe of Seven—Bob, Rhonda, Jim, Marilyn, Mike, Janice, Donna and the members of my Canadian Authors Association, Peterborough Branch. Also, second cousin Cindy, met through DNA testing.

Thanks also to Prim Pemberton and the individuals who participated in her workshops, *Creative Writing in Cabbagetown*. They critiqued and offered suggestions and encouragement along the way: Barb Nahwegahbow, Josie Mounsey, Ilene Cummings, Sylvie Daigneault, Ann Bjorseth, Mel James, Philip Jessup, Lindsay Ure, Pippa Domville, Mary Bennett.

Our guide, Malcolm Handoll guided us through the intricacies of the Orkney Islands.

Especially, I wish to thank my wife, Donna, who is included in most of the groups above as my greatest friend, supporter, advisor, and editor throughout the process of writing this story.

Also I would like to offer special thanks for their advice to Eileen Dunne and Alan E. Dunne.

Certainly, it has been a pleasure working with FriesenPress for the second time with special thanks to my Publishing Specialist, Carly Cumpstone.

Also by J. Stephen Thompson

Novels
The Aftermath
Lincoln Cathedral

Editing & Reissuing
Bomber Crew, Second Edition
by Jack E. Thompson

Photography
Reflections Through a Special Lens:
The Photography of Jack E. Thompson

Collaborative Novel
Tales from the Raven Café—with various authors

Anthologies
Kawartha Soul Project—with authors from
the Canadian Authors, Peterborough Branch

Kawartha Imagination Project—with authors from
the Canadian Authors, Peterborough Branch

Kawartha Lakes Stories, Autumn—with authors
from Kawartha Lakes Writers

To my wife, Donna

To my children and their partners, Ondine & Rod, Michael,
Alex & Catherine, Bryce & Darlanne, and Graham

To my grandchildren and their partners, Emiline & Adam,
Nicholas & Stacey, William & Audrey

To my great-grandchildren, Gavin, Austin, and Mylah

Dramatis Personae

Marchesa di Mentone	Toronto Blue Jays fan. Her life story is subject of the narrative. Also known as Marsha
Tommaso	Father of Marchesa
Drago	Italian-American prison guard in Italian POW camp. Marchesa's guide through Europe at the conclusion of World War II
Edmondo	Italian Prison guard
Gregor Andrew MacGregor	Andy. Marchesa's husband
Ben	Proprietor of My Spot restaurant
Richard Dixon	Sports journalist
Chantal Jefferson	Sports journalist
Leanne, Ross, Nate, Simon, Charlene, David	My Spot restaurant regulars
Jorge	My Spot regular. Also known as George
Mike Davies	Andy's Ottawa friend
Sally	My Spot server
Dave	Toronto police detective. Richard's childhood friend
Hank Barton	Ottawa journalist. Richard's colleague
Ross family	Marchesa's adoptive parents in Edinburgh
Brian & William Georgas	Richard's half-brothers identified by DNA testing
Abigaille Giovani	Marchesa's mother
Albertina di Mentone	Marchesa's sister
Alessandros Audisio	Also known as Sandros. Boston Red Sox first baseman
Pierre	Ottawa hospital pharmacist

1

ITALY 1945

"*Affrettatevi figlia! Adesso!*" Marchesa heard and understood her father's instructions. "It is good it is raining. Drago said he cut the fence so we can get out. Hurry Marchesa. *Mamma e Albertina sono andati prima.*"

Twelve-year-old Marchesa di Mentone moved slowly over the slick mud surface of the prison compound. She stepped cautiously, carefully planting each individual step, trying to maintain her balance. She progressed as quickly as possible in the direction her father had pointed. She advanced blindly, fighting to keep her eyes at least partially open in the driving rain. A lightning flash briefly illuminated the line of about three dozen people slipping toward a gap in the fence. She was certain the German guards would see them with the sky so lit up. Later when she caught up to her mother and sister, she thought about how they'd been led out from their compound in the Trieste prison by the only two remaining Italian guards, they themselves escaping their German commanders. Edmondo and Drago had become friendly with her father, Tommaso, often furtively conversing in one of the two blind corners of the enclosure where they determined they'd be concealed from the sightlines of the watchtower.

"What do you discuss, Pappa," Marchesa asked her father.

"Nothing and everything. They're Italian too," Tommaso answered.

She thought there must be more to it, the way they hid themselves from view. She felt slighted by his answer, but even at her young age, she knew better than to persist.

"Be careful not to draw the attention of the guards." Tommaso was suspicious of everyone.

So, what is Pappa planning with these men? Marchesa thought. *They have been our jailers for many, many months.*

While she was watching, she thought of earlier times when she watched her father as he held stand-up meetings in secluded spots in Bergamo, often in a park, with two or three other men. Even at that younger age, her focus was on how to accomplish things, and she understood her father to be accomplished. So, she scrutinised him.

Tommaso had been elected mayor of the Lombardy city of Bergamo as a member of the Communist Party. That did not seem to pose a problem at the time. Later, her father became a political prisoner, arrested along with his wife, Abigaille and two daughters, Marchesa and her younger sister, Albertina. To the Mussolini Fascists they were undesirables. They had been interned originally at Màntova.

After the 1943 Italian armistice, German forces removed the whole POW population of disloyal Italian military personnel and civilians to Trieste, away from the Allied forces advancing from Southern Italy.

∼

"Stay with Drago," her father said when he caught up with her. "He will take us to meet Yugoslav Partisans across the border in Slovenia. Stay together. I need to go back now. I will catch up with you later. I know the way." Tommaso patted Marchesa on the shoulder.

"But Pappa, please stay with me now."

"Go with Drago. Stay close. I must go back."

∼

In the slippery and progressively rougher terrain, she quickly became separated from her mother and sister. She tried to stay calm. She understood they must stay quiet. In the camp, she had overheard rumours about the end of the war being imminent. But she seemed to know they would be treated like escaped criminals if they were recaptured.

Drago guided her to safety. He found her dry places to sit and wait while he repeatedly retraced their route to reconnoitre, to locate other escaped prisoners, and to search for her family. The more time passed, the more she accepted the reality of their separation.

Drago, this middle-aged man, attended to her needs as he would with his own daughter. Marchesa eventually learned he was raised Italian but of Serbian heritage. His parents left the strife-bound Balkan peninsula with their young son for the employment opportunities of Italy. Years later, even as Mussolini came to power, they still preferred him to what they heard of the increasingly dictatorial King Alexander in embryonic Yugoslavia. They considered it a blessing that their son should be raised Italian.

Marchesa's parents had never discussed family origins. During their imprisonment, they were careful not to share personal information with anyone including their young daughters. So, when Drago now suggested she, like him, might be Yugoslav, Marchesa was taken aback.

"Di Mentone is an Italian name." She stared directly at Drago as if to ask what was wrong with him.

"Di Mentone is from Poe."

"Who?"

"Edgar Allan Poe the American poet."

"Oh." Marchesa did not feel enlightened.

2

Drago led Marchesa through the hills of Slovenia. He was intent on avoiding retreating German forces. He was particularly concerned with encountering unorganized groups or rogue individuals not ready to accept impending defeat. At the same time, although his purpose was to keep her safe, he encouraged her to remain on the lookout for her family. That he did to help keep her focussed. He was determined to outlast this ordeal. As much as Drago liked Tommaso, reunification of the di Mentone family was not uppermost on his mind. His and Marchesa's survival was. Catch up with the others later after things inevitably settled down. In the meantime, he felt that remaining unencumbered was their best bet. He had come to appreciate Marchesa's intelligence, easy manner, and stubborn tenacity. Whether they walked ten, twenty, or thirty kilometres in a day did not seem to disconcert her, nor did she require or want a day of rest after a long trek. She seemed to be as focussed as Drago himself.

They travelled in a small group as they proceeded through Slovenia into Croatia. Drago had become their acknowledged leader. He would send men he trusted to gather intelligence from other groups of refugees on an almost daily basis. He tried to keep Marchesa hidden from other migrant groups and them from her. Somehow, he was always able to scrounge food or find a safe place to rest or sleep.

This day, however, Marchesa thought Drago seemed flustered, uncharacteristically unsure of himself. She watched him glance down—at the ground, at his boots. Marchesa thought his face seemed flushed. When he eventually looked up, he regained his usual eye contact with her.

"Little one, please, sit here. I need to talk to you." He pointed toward the largest stone beside the path. "This is going to be difficult."

Marchesa had not seen Drago so nervous. In the time she'd known him, he always appeared confident. She sat as told. "What is it?" she asked.

They were speaking English. Drago had insisted early on. "It will be our secret language," he explained to Marchesa. "No one will understand here in Croatia. That way we cannot be in danger for something we say."

Marchesa knew nothing of the language before they started to converse in English, but she picked up the everyday vocabulary necessary for their conversations quickly and easily.

Drago knew English. He told Marchesa he'd lived about twenty years in America but returned to Italy in 1940 while America was still nominally neutral in the war.

"America seemed like it would join the war very soon," he explained. "If they did that, I was afraid I would be treated as a bad American. No *immigrato* should be considered an enemy in their new land. But they didn't know me."

"You lived there a long time."

"Actually, I lived there longer than I lived in Italy. But I was worried. You know about living in a prison camp. That was not going to be for me." He told her about his cousin in Canada who had been arrested almost immediately after Canada joined the war.

"I know you understand about prison camps, but I don't know

what you understand about other things like immigration. You are so young to be in this situation. I don't think you know about enemy aliens."

"How do you know so much, Drago?"

"Reading, mostly—books, newspapers—listening, watching. You must learn something new every day, little one."

She understood what Drago meant about learning new things.

Now Drago switched to Italian. "Little one, I'm sorry. There is no easy way to say this." He held her close and said softly, "Edmondo heard something about your father. He is very brave. He protected you. Now he has left his life to you. He is a hero."

Marchesa sat, stunned. Her eyes widened, and her jaw sagged until she understood what Drago had stated and cried, "Pappa? How?"

Drago explained that Edmondo had heard from a group of migrants that Tommaso had been shot. Executed. Rumoured to have been transported to a Yugoslav concentration camp. Executed in one of the infamous killing fields along with former Fascists and Nazi collaborators.

Marchesa bent over sobbing. Drago touched her shoulder, and as she slumped toward him, hugged her.

"Poor Pappa. Poor Mamma and Albertina. Do you think Mamma and Albertina know? We need to find them so I can explain to Albertina."

Drago said that Marchesa's mother and sister could be in a refugee camp, possibly still in Slovenia. "But I really have no reason to know where they might be. I just don't know," he answered Marchesa.

"We need to find them. What will they do…how will they live without Pappa?" *How will Albertina live without me*—povera sorellina. *Mamma was not well in the camp. I looked after my sister,* she thought.

"We will continue to look, but, little one, for now we are better to keep to ourselves. Do your feet still hurt?" Drago suggested they move on, maybe to Sarajevo. "North-western Yugoslavia seems to be in chaos. Unorganized, uncoordinated, unfocussed, and too many other refugees."

"We should leave this area," he said. "You may not understand what I'm saying, little one. What I have been seeing makes me think no one is in charge. It looks like anarchy."

∼

"What did you do in America, Drago?"

"I was a policeman." Drago paused. "I was sixteen when I arrived in America. My father sent me there to work in my uncle's bakery. It's a place called Boston."

"A policeman?"

"Well, my uncle said I was too young not to go to school. He insisted I help only with the early morning bread baking. He kept pushing me to go to school as well."

"I want to go to school also. That would make Pappa happy." She tried to stifle her renewed sobbing. After a moment she asked, "What happened?"

"When I came back to Italy it was after twenty years away. I thought I was too old to be a soldier. And," Drago whispered, "I didn't want to fight. I volunteered to be a guard in a prisoner-of-war camp."

"Why?" Marchesa was always curious.

Drago seemed to understand that inquisitiveness could take her far if he could extract her from this chaotic destruction. He knew America would be physically unhurt. He understood intuitively it would necessitate patient perseverance for him to get back there, let alone take her with him.

He took his time answering her query. "I knew I needed to do something for my country."

"Was Italy still your country? Is Italy my country? They didn't want us."

"I am American but Italian first. The 1914 war didn't disturb me so much because America and Italy were friends. I was just a kid then. What did I know?" He quickly looked at Marchesa, seeming to realize how his *just a kid* remark might affect her.

3

TORONTO 2013

Marchesa walked along Front Street until she turned north along Spadina. As she proceeded, she reminisced about when she explored this route for the first time. How uneasy she had been to encounter a different part of the city. How she quickly came to prefer the restricted space of Baldwin Street to the width of Spadina Avenue. How now, it had become her destination of choice. How she appreciated the contrast. How the shops that spilled out onto the street had begun to seem exciting. Sidewalk clothing racks protected from weather risks by awnings of different sizes, strengths, and colours. Small grocerias with outdoor produce bins, haphazard ledge projections, large tubs of beautiful tomatoes, green peppers, green onions, and interesting, pink warty fruit she didn't recognize.

She thought that next time, she might like to investigate the other side of the street. Yet she was pleased to be strolling in the morning sunshine on the west side of Spadina.

She recalled how relieved she'd been to chance onto Baldwin Street. She now thought it must have been Spadina's traffic that bothered her, the panorama of vehicle lanes, the mid-road transit corridor. Today she surveyed the young trees planted alongside the streetcar tracks. *It will be quite beautiful in a few years*, she thought. And that brought her to think that she and her late husband Andy had discussed how municipal projects owed it to their people to be attractive or charming as well as functional. The street wasn't particularly busy today.

She'd been living in Toronto for more than a year but had only recently decided to get out to investigate neighbourhoods. Andy had always convinced her to cherish and seek out local landmarks such as Kensington Market or St Lawrence Market in addition to the usual historic and tourist sites. But now Andy was dead—not here to guide her. She was on her own. She needed to learn to live and cherish her own life without his support and guidance. Even though his death was certainly not unanticipated, she missed him so much. Once in a while, including today, she sensed an ugly specter telling her she would be investigated for complicity in his death. She was now tilting toward convincing herself that enough time had passed; she could live without that fear and allow herself to wander around downtown Toronto.

She was transported to a more comfortable place when recalling Andy speaking with her.

"Really, Marki," Andy would say, "a city is defined by its neighbourhoods, not by its institutions."

"Aren't outdoor markets surprising in Canadian cities? The season is so short."

"Perhaps not as short as you think. I expect they're here to stay."

On first arriving in Canada, she'd been surprised to find what she considered holdovers from older cultures in an otherwise modern country. She'd left behind one such culture, a feature of recovery in war-torn Europe. Not that she was so naïve as to expect streets paved in gold.

When they lived in Ottawa, Andy cajoled Marchesa to visit the Ottawa Farmer's Market. Eventually, that became something they did every Sunday. Marchesa soon came to enjoy wandering amongst the shops and restaurants of Byward Market as well. She came to observe that this was the purview of the middle and upper middle class. Fresh and specialty food was not inexpensive. This was not the necessity of recovery. She was never certain how this fit with economist Andy's international trade philosophies. When she kidded him that she couldn't rationalize his thinking with his conduct, he would say, "Lass, 'tis the weekend."

Today she realized this was what she had become comfortable with—stalls stretching out onto the sidewalk. Tables piled with goods—some carelessly, others fastidiously symmetrical. She felt content walking around here. She still shopped at The Bay and Holt Renfrew and fondly remembered the times Andy took her to Harrods while they still lived in the UK. That was after they'd been married awhile. In her first years in the UK, wartime rationing was still firmly in place.

Then her mind returned her to Baldwin Street. Her easy pace belied her age. In fact, she realized she would arrive at the café earlier than usual, if usual was an apt term to describe a habit she was still only just developing.

She'd found My Spot restaurant quite accidentally. The clean lines of the exterior of the café and the large windows drew her in, even though graffiti covered the blue pillars edging the storefront and the outside bench seat. Nothing offensive but garish, nonetheless. Why the bold double letters as if no one could read the smaller ones?

When she pulled out her camera, a woman seated inside the restaurant at a window table scowled, stood up, and moved further back into the interior. Marchesa was surprised, hesitated briefly, but looked through the viewfinder and shot the photo anyway.

She knew there were many breakfast places nearer her retirement condo. Even the dining room in the assisted living section in her own building was okay, although it provided little choice. She did not want to see herself as needing supported care, and, besides, she was tired of the limited menu. Still acceptable when reserved for emergencies such as pouring rain or unshovelled winter sidewalks. Every other place she'd tried had been acceptable, but she preferred such things as a *mélange* of fresh seasonal fruits and berries, not just a perennial collection of melon chunks in or out of season. She had no problem with freshly harvested, locally grown melons but didn't appreciate them as a year-round staple.

As long as the weather was clement, she preferred to be outside. In fact, she'd discovered the wonderful sidewalk cafés of Montreal nearly forty years past, especially her favourites in old Montreal, replete with flowering plants and serious attention to the preparation of excellent coffees. She missed those wonderful places for a morning coffee. Since that time, she'd promised to treat herself to breakfast—coffee and pastries—whenever she could. Years later, when they moved from Montreal to Ottawa, that was still an easy promise to keep. Now in Toronto, she'd tried several of the cafés along Queen's Quay, even several of the hotels and the ubiquitous Tim Hortons and Starbucks. What she really wanted was a properly prepared double espresso. Surely that shouldn't be so hard to find. Now, she approached her chosen café, My Spot, this Monday morning.

"You're early today." The young man moved out from behind the counter to greet her.

"You are open?" Marchesa looked toward the lighted OPEN sign in the window.

"Yes, of course," he said. "We open at six-thirty. Would you like your usual?"

"My usual?"

"Double espresso, Kenya double A."

Marchesa smiled at the man, pleased to be recognized but not certain she wished to be categorized by preferred coffee type. "Yes," she said. "The usual."

Maybe I should be perverse and order a macchiato or latté. But that young man is pleasant.

She wished she could remember his name. She thought to look at his name tag, but he'd already moved away to prepare her coffee. *One of the regulars called him Ken, or was that Ben?*

She didn't like to be classified. As a bioethicist, she'd fought labelling most of her life and was surprised when she slipped and applied tags to other people herself. *Regulars, how would I know?* She laughed softly, actually, hardly a laugh just a slight smile and a barely audible *hmm*.

On her first visit, she had expanded her usual early morning walking route to include much of Kensington Market. She'd heard of the area so often during her frequent visits to Toronto with Andy. Andy loved Toronto and often expressed a wish to have season's tickets for the Blue Jays. Before his health deteriorated. Before she'd decided to move here.

That first day, she'd stepped through the door into this bustling restaurant. She was taken aback by how narrow the space seemed. And she couldn't see an available table. Ben approached her with the suggestion that she sit at the end of the long table just opposite the counter. It'd obviously been fashioned by shoving three tables together. She'd objected when she realized he meant to place her at a large but occupied table. Six patrons were already seated.

"No, no," Marchesa said, "I don't want to bother anybody."

"It won't be a bother," Ben insisted. "We're friendly."

This particular Monday morning, she sat at the same table in the seat she preferred because no one else was in the café when she arrived. She faced the door as she always tried to do ever since Drago had taught her to always be aware. Closer to eight o'clock, others started to arrive. She recognized some from her previous visits. So far, she'd only come here a few weekdays, never on a weekend.

Eventually, there were seven others seated around the table, all who greeted her with shy nods. She looked away from her table companions and focussed on the display case atop the counter, the bright yellow walls and the two staff behind the counter busily preparing coffee and tea orders. *Tea? In the morning? Don't get me started on that.* As far as she could tell, the café did not have a stale beer smell, so she decided it didn't transform into a bar later in the day.

Then she looked at the people around her. She was certain she'd seen that woman close to the door around Queen's Quay or on Front Street sometime. Probably on one of her regular walks. Maybe near that boutique hotel around the corner from the CBC building.

Marchesa self-consciously moved her right hand onto her lap to steady her tremor. She'd forced herself to learn to use her left hand for minor movements once she realized she was having trouble controlling her right. Though, she'd hardly become left-handed. That would be quite a struggle, but her logical mind recognized this was likely a progressive condition and not transitory. Eventually, she projected negatively, it could lead to having trouble controlling her whole right side. However, her emotional brain was just not ready to accept that concept. So, for the moment, she was concerned with hiding her shakiness from friends and colleagues in stressful and unusual situations.

Marchesa watched other customers greet the staff and each other as they came through the door. She was beginning to realize it wasn't just the newly familiar seven who were regulars.

Everyone seems to know everyone else. But they each arrive separately. A meeting place.

Rather like her seats at the baseball stadium. Everyone in her section greeted each other. Here, it probably had developed simply as a well-established morning routine.

She looked back at the woman seated at the low counter in front of the window. What caught her attention was a brief snippet she overheard, a phrase muttered to show displeasure. *Not my idear*, she thought she heard.

If I heard what I think I heard I would guess New England. Probably Boston. Not that she considered herself a dialectologist or philologist. Far from it — just a hobby from her time at Oxford. Something she played with. She found she got along better in Montreal when she dropped her BBC English and replaced it with a slight Italian accent. The accent she'd fought so hard to abandon. Certainly, it worked well shopping on Sainte Catherine West. With so much vocabulary similar to Italian she learned French easily. Her ability to learn languages had served her well in life. In Montreal, she used French in the cafés and the little shops with the exquisite clothing lines. Poor Andy trying to be understood when he spoke French — he had the vocabulary but just couldn't lose his Scottish accent, whatever he tried.

Thinking about it now amused her. She remembered when they were still living in Edinburgh, hearing Andy deal with some workmen at the door of their flat. Andy had adapted well to, in her mind, the soft, almost lilting Edinburgh accent. But in speaking with the men who were there to fix some problem with their windows, he had taken on an emphasized Glaswegian vernacular. Marchesa understood almost nothing of what was said. When she asked him about it later, Andy shrugged and told her that with workmen, he needed to drop pretense to ensure a good job.

Life was so hard without Andy. That was why she'd chosen to move to Toronto where she could make her own fresh start. It'd been so difficult continuing to live in Ottawa after his death. Everything so familiar yet so foreign without him by her side. So many questions from the police about her possible role in his death. Even the well-meant offered condolences made her uncomfortable.

Andy had become well known, especially amongst climate change advocates and in University of Ottawa circles after his years of teaching and researching there. And, of course, there were the two novels he'd written. Even when he turned to fiction, his writing of *Osprey* and *Minor to Major* was heavily influenced by geography and economics.

Now Marchesa would have preferred to sit at a small table, so anyone who sat beside her would be of her own choosing. But she was glad she'd chosen to live downtown, pleased she could afford her retirement condo but unsure how long she'd stay. Pleased that medical care could be available. She was beginning to be not unhappy, perhaps at least content, with her independence. She didn't require any of the available increased care yet. As she moved her right hand onto her lap to steady it, or at least hide her shake, she knew it could become necessary in the future. She had been diagnosed. Essential Tremor. A diagnosis was simply another label. What would make it essential? Who would attach such a sardonic reference to a tremor?

4

Richard Dixon stood, stretched forward to the edge of the press box. He wanted to confirm where and at whom he supposed Chantal Jefferson was pointing. "So, Chantal, you said behind home plate?"

"In the stands, just behind…"

"Okay then." He extended himself further. "You mean directly below?"

"C'mon, Dickie, pay attention. I already told you. She's the woman in…let's see…"

Richard grinned at being called Dickie. *The only Dickie here is R.A. Dickey*, he thought and laughed, but he didn't say that. He inclined his head toward the pitcher's mound and nodded several times as he regarded the spot where the Blue Jays knuckleballer would take command for the next half inning. None of Richard's colleagues called him Dickie. He had assiduously avoided a nickname, especially after his high school days when he'd often been called Dickhead or worse—automatic juvenile appellations for someone with the surname Dixon. By his senior year, most of the jocks simply called him Dix. His slight stature meant he wasn't built for most high school team sports, but he could play baseball exceptionally well—pitcher or shortstop were his preferred positions, but he was always willing to take any position the coach needed him to play. He was remarkably quick and would enthusiastically accept any occasion to play.

Richard was how he introduced himself, no contractions or diminutives.

Chantal pointed to the seats. "The woman in the second row."

"They call those *In the Action* seats." Richard's view was partially blocked by the short wall that delineated the section. "That's my kind of action—wait staff, snacks and elbow bending. I could go for that. And right behind home plate."

"We can't really complain about our view from here, though."

Chantal shrugged as she considered the press box, then pointed to the television monitors on the wall behind them. "Watch when the batter's in place. Camera straight on from centre field."

Richard moved closer to the TV screen. He pointed to a middle-aged woman leaning toward and talking to a man beside her. "Is that who you're talking about?"

"No, the older woman to her left...no, right. Her right, your left. Right on the left-hand side of the second row. Okay, look now—straight into the stands behind a left-handed batter." She hesitated before she spoke again. "You've never noticed her before?"

"I don't really take the time to watch baseball on TV. And, of course, never watch the Jays. I suppose you'd find that ironic?"

Chantal didn't respond. They both continued to stare. Guessed her to be in her seventies. Grey hair, smartly attired in a dress and a perfectly matching Sierra blue accent scarf. Not your usual Jays garb. The camera angle changed so quickly it was hard to capture details.

Then Richard's attention was interrupted. The crowd cheered as the ball flew deep into centre field. Caught on a flying dive. A collective moan, and the fans collapsed back into their seats.

"Good thing that wasn't a dinger. You had me distracted there," he said. "Anyway, whadda'ya want to know?"

"Who is she?" She looked directly at Richard. "I can't recall when I first noticed her, but she's so there when I watch the monitors. She must have season tickets because she's there for almost every game. Sometimes she has someone with her. She's got my interest. I find myself looking for her. I actually miss her when she's not there."

Richard paid attention to what Chantal was saying. He was interested and puzzled. If Chantal's observations were so obvious, the woman could have an interesting story. Everyone has a story. But he didn't want to speculate. He'd built his career on *just the facts ma'am*, as he often joked.

Chantal motioned back toward the TV. She grinned. "Now that you've see her from that camera angle, you'll understand. I call her home plate lady."

Richard looked again, scrutinized the television screen with an expression of realization. He shook his head.

Richard said nothing more, nor did Chantal goad him. He was back at the game, surveying the field, then began to type on his laptop.

Lady behind home plate, he wrote in his notes.

～

"Richard," Ben said. "Welcome back. Haven't seen you in a while."

"It hasn't been that long, Ben." Richard moved toward the middle table in the restaurant, toward the seat he'd come to think of as his.

"You been on assignment?"

Richard shook his head. "Nah. Just busy. A lot of late games, so I haven't been anxious to get going in the morning. Need my beauty sleep, eh?"

"Gotcha. The usual then?" Ben didn't really need to ask. He knew Richard was the black and strong, nothing fancy, just good coffee.

Richard greeted the others at the main table and nodded to some of the those customers seated at other tables around the room. He didn't sit immediately but approached Ben at the service counter.

"Can't wait, I see." Ben often spoke with familiarity with his long-term customers, his regulars. "You need that jolt right away?"

Richard laughed, then spoke quietly. "The older lady—Marsha, is it?" Ben nodded. "What do you know about her?"

"Basically nothing," Ben replied. "She comes in maybe a couple times a week."

"How long has she been doing that?"

"Oh, I don't know, several months, I guess. Why?"

"Don't know. Reminds me of someone. Just wondering."

5

Chantal glanced toward Richard's desk and saw he was engrossed with something on his laptop, so she didn't say anything that might interrupt him. She read his columns regularly. She was always impressed with his complete comprehension of the game and portrayals of the action, especially his analysis of swing mechanics that develop into a home run. That one-eighth of a second. A coordinated series of contractions — muscles, joints, connective tissues — from the kinetics to the hands, and ultimately, to the bat. The stance, the stride, the swing plane and follow through.

She found him to be a steadying motivational influence from the first day she'd arrived on the scene. She — the new sports columnist, and female to boot. Not a rookie in either the newspaper business or in sports reporting. The difference: now she was charged with a column, an opinion piece. Still, she had the impression she needed to prove herself before she was accepted or even tolerated by the male press box. She had watched as they took off immediately once the outcome of games was determined. Deadlines, she did understand. But Richard was the first of the group to take the time even to introduce himself.

Chantal had been ready for a change, to try something new a year ago when she was approached to step into this freshly created sports columnist position. She'd been back in Toronto, and frankly, was worn out from twelve years as a foreign correspondent. Starting with postwar Kosovo and the continuing Balkan crises, then eventually moving on to assume Middle East assignments. She needed a break. Her thoughts and dreams no longer haunted, but disturbed her.

It's not that she hadn't reported on sports. Her first assignment was the Turin Olympics. She suspected it had been a financial decision. She was already working in Southeastern Europe and able to move easily over to Italy even for just the several weeks necessary to cover the Olympic and Paralympic period. At the time, it gave her a much-needed break. Much to her delight, her second Olympics assignment in Vancouver was offered because of the great job she'd done in Turin.

Winter sports were certainly within her sphere of experience. As a competitive downhill racer, she was excruciatingly close to qualifying for the national Olympic ski team — actually, within one competitor of making it. A fraction of a second in time and space. Chantal knew sports, individual sports rather than team sports, understood the dedication of elite athletes and knew the disappointment of not being selected, of being one of the top in the world but still not making it.

In her calm moments, Chantal appreciated that her new position had been designed specifically with her in mind.

"You looking forward to Boston coming in next week?" Richard suddenly asked.

"Yes!" Chantal's shoulders tightened at being consulted. "They always give the Jays a good run. I get so into the game that I really don't sleep well until they leave town."

"How about when you're in Boston?" Richard asked.

"You may think I'm crazy, but I don't have the same problem there. I love Boston...always so much to do and see. I just enjoy the city. Here, this is home. That make sense?"

"Sure, I get what you're saying," Richard said. He paused, then continued to talk. "What do you think of their new acquisitions? How about Audisio?"

She shook her head, although she did know who he was talking about. She was merely surprised Richard would ask for her opinion. That had not been her experience in the time she'd known him.

"The new Red Sox guy. First base."

"Yeah, I know, I know. He'll...uh...he'll be good once he's made a few starts." *There*, she thought, *slipping back into sports jargon when I have no idea what to say.*

"I've booked an interview with him before Friday's game. He made a few good outs last time they played here. Even salvaged a couple of bobbles. You know, throwing errors from third, but he recovered the ball to make the outs."

"Where'd he come from, anyway?" Chantal asked. "I don't remember ever seeing him play last season."

"Last year, he was still playing in Japan. Before that, the Chinese professional leagues."

"Pardon me? Chinese professional leagues? Those exist?"

"Ah, Chantal, so much to learn. Baseball is very popular in China." Richard laughed, then said, "Truth is, I only learned about the Chinese leagues after Audisio was picked up by Boston. Apparently very good calibre."

"What's your interest in Boston players?"

"I think it's a Toronto thing. Like hockey," Richard said. "Toronto fans...always interested in what Montreal is up to. And that extends to other close rivals like the Bruins."

"I guess I know what you're saying. But why him, this Audisio?"

It was Richard's turn to shrug. "His name interested me. Audisio sounds like a Latin American name, but he looks so European. And for someone to be this good, why haven't we seen him in the minors?"

"Good point."

"So, I researched it. He may have played in Japan and China, but I understand he's Italian."

6

Ben approached Marchesa and asked quietly whether she would like another double espresso.

Marchesa was enjoying this morning. She loved the assortment of aromas in the restaurant — fresh coffee, hot baking fresh from the oven and the general good smells of breakfasts made on the grill. She would definitely like another drink but wondered whether more espresso might exaggerate her tremor.

"I think a macchiato now." She wasn't certain of the comparative caffeine levels but had decided to stay a while longer. "And do you have fresh pastries this morning?" *That might be a stretch on a Monday morning*, she thought. He assured her the pastries were fresh and left to get an assortment for her to choose from. She knew it was something of a Greek restaurant. She didn't want baklava at this time of day, but she thought she could trust Ben's judgement to come up with her sort of breakfast.

Before he returned with her macchiato and a tray of pastries, Ben kibitzed with one of the customers.

As Ben moved back toward her, the man continued to walk in reverse gear toward the door, talking to Ben at the same time.

"I gotta leave. I gotta leave now," he finally said. The others at the table shook their heads as they watched. She realized this patter was likely to be a recurring vignette.

That first day, when he had placed her at that table, Ben had said, "This is Marsha." He quickly named the others seated there for her benefit. She was not certain what he'd called that man. She knew they'd been introduced, yet he reminded her of someone completely different, someone from somewhere else.

"This morning, we have nice mini-baguettes served with cheese." Ben interrupted her thoughts. "And," he continued, "these almond croissants are excellent. Also, my very favourite, apple tarte Tatin." She chose a slice of the tarte and two of the biscotti he hadn't mentioned. She was pleased the Tatin had been properly inverted from the pie plate, so what she focussed on was the suitably caramelized apples rather than the pastry topping.

Although she had begun to feel more relaxed now that she had visited the restaurant more frequently, still she watched the door, a habit she'd never been able to shake. Drago had taught her to always know who and what was around her — for her own safety and the security of the group of people she might be with. She felt safe living first in Britain, then Canada, but some tendencies never leave. Her glances toward the door still allowed her to observe the others at the table. She couldn't see the men at the far end of the counter very well, but they seemed to be conversing. The men and women at the side tables in front of the washroom door appeared to know each other well. It was only the woman with the Boston accent who didn't seem to interact with anyone. Marchesa decided to speak to her. She looked rather lonely.

"Are you from Boston?" she asked.

The woman raised her eyebrows. "You talking to me?"

"Yes, I wondered if you are from Boston."

"Yeah," the woman replied with a *what's it to ya* scowl.

"Do you come here often?" Marchesa mentally kicked herself for that weak assertion. *Of course, I don't know her. I've only been here a few times myself.* But she wasn't ready to give up. She would like to talk with someone who was not from where she lived. Someone younger. Some conversation not involving health care.

"My name's Marsha," she began again. She'd finally taken

Andy's surname and his diminutive for her. She thought Marsha MacGregor would play better in an Ontario city. Her di Mentone surname, although simple to her, had proved quite a nuisance. She always needed to spell it for people, repeatedly. So, she made the conscious makeover decision to be Marsha MacGregor in Toronto. She didn't know yet whether she would change her name on her health card, and it didn't matter beyond that because she'd voluntarily given up her driver's licence. That was her one acknowledgement of the possibility of a protracted neurological affliction.

"Leanne," the woman replied.

"Pleased to meet you, Leanne."

"You were the one taking pictures the other week."

"Right." Marchesa paused. "Oh, I'm so sorry. That would have been you in the window. I didn't really look inside. I was concentrated on the building and its unusual character. I don't believe in taking photos of individuals in public when I don't know them."

"We live here," Leanne said. "Then all you tourists come and examine our lives. As if we're…I dunno…zoo animals, I guess."

"I'm not a tourist," Marchesa said defensively.

Leanne stared at her.

"I live nearby."

Leanne looked Marchesa up and down, as if assessing her smartly tailored navy-blue dress complemented with an off-white scarf. Then she turned away to face the window.

Marchesa shook her head in amusement. *So much for engaging her in conversation.*

Two more patrons came in. One took the seat beside Leanne, and the second claimed the seat between the two men at the other end of the long table. She realized it was foolish, but she felt that any addition to the original group was an encroachment of some sort, a violation. She gestured to Ben to make up her bill as she hurriedly finished her slice of tarte.

I shouldn't rush eating. It causes my indigestion. I don't want to go back on meds. She remembered reading somewhere that upsetting the fragile balance of stomach acids could lead to more acute tremors. Normally, she wouldn't accept something that could be considered anecdotal or junk science, but she was captivated when it was something potentially affecting her own well-being.

She left enough money on the counter to cover her bill and what she considered a generous tip. The staff at My Spot didn't look like students, but throughout her long academic career, she felt an obligation to tip well, knowing how many wait staff were putting themselves through school. She herself had always had scholarship support right from her secondary school equivalency studies in the UK. She consequently never had to work in a café.

After leaving the café, she continued west on Baldwin, enjoying the beautiful sunny June day. Perfect for poking around in the shops and stalls. Maybe she'd come upon something different for dinner like she and Andy used to do when they strolled through Ottawa's Byward Market.

Andy, she thought, *this is your kind of day.*

7

Later that week, Marchesa was back in what had now become her accustomed seat at My Spot.

She glanced toward the café door. She'd been distracted, daydreaming. Had let her guard down. She looked straight at Leanne, who had slipped in when she hadn't been aware.

She was somewhat startled that she'd been abnormally inattentive, allowing Leanne to sneak in unnoticed. Following their escape long ago, Drago had continually impressed upon her to always be vigilant, constantly aware. She knew she had slipped today and felt embarrassed.

"Good morning, Leanne," she said, aiming to sound cheerful.

"Oh, hi...umm..."

"Marsha," Marchesa said. She looked back to the doorway as one of the men who usually sat at the other end of the table came through, started toward his usual spot, then suddenly caught her eye and moved toward her, taking her attention away from a kind of embarrassing attempt to engage with Leanne.

"Hello, Marsha, I'm Ross," he said as he leaned in with his hands on the back of the empty chair between the two women. "I've been thinking you look familiar to me—like I should know you, but for the life of me, I can't place from where. I have an antique store on Queen West. Crown Antiques. Maybe you've been in the store?"

Well, there's a conversation starter. She smiled because she'd expected some obligatory weather talk. She realized she'd misjudged him. *Ross,* she reminded herself. *I don't know about this. I'm trying to get Leanne to open up, yet I don't want to myself.*

"No," she said. "I don't think I've been there."

"So that's not it," Ross said. "Must be something else."

"Tell me where your shop is."

"I can do better than that." Ross extracted his wallet from the back pocket of his tight pants. "Here's my address." He flipped his business card through his fingers as adroitly as a cardsharp. "There's a map on the back side. That's exactly where I am."

"Maybe I'll come see you then."

"Are you interested in antiques?"

"My husband and I collected a few pieces. Mostly from Europe. Of no specific vintage."

She was thinking of their desks from Scotland. And the old Quebec dining room pieces. Probably European originally. Fine things, things made by craftsmen, no particular region or age. She laughed and said, "In fact, Andy used to say the only important vintage was in wine. And, of course, Scotch whisky."

"Andy would be your husband, I assume," Ross said. "These days, maybe that's quite an assumption."

Marchesa could feel her face reddening. This was getting personal. "My late husband," she replied.

"Oh. Sorry to be so flip."

"It'll soon be two years—just before Christmas." She didn't know why she impulsively added that detail. "It still feels so fresh."

I so don't want to talk about this. But I need to do something about my storage locker. I don't want anyone to know Andy's name. Maybe then the police would want to reopen the case and find a suspicious death.

"That time of year makes it tough for families."

Marchesa didn't respond. She and Andy had decided not to have children. They realized once his parents and siblings passed, they'd be alone in the world, hers not having survived the war. They quite enjoyed it that way. Her life had been wonderful from the time Drago managed to find a way to get her across the English Channel and into the UK.

She paused and chose her words. "A stroke. He didn't suffer." She surprised herself with her uncharacteristic ease of sharing the story she and Andy had agreed upon. She seemed to need to say something.

"Sorry to hear that," one of the other men said. "I know Ben introduced us all, but we haven't really talked. I'm Nate."

Marchesa remembered Ben's quick introductions when she'd first come to My Spot. Ben himself and Sally, the server, then Ross, Nate, maybe Richard, she wasn't sure whether he'd mentioned Leanne at the time. She still didn't remember the names of the other usuals or casual staff. *Funny*, she thought, *I've reached the point where I recognize them all, but I'm embarrassed to admit I don't know their names since so much time has passed.*

"Just so you know, Marsha," Nate continued, "our table regulars are being treated by yours truly today. Enjoy your espresso."

"Thank you, but it's not necessary to include me."

"Ah, but it is. It's my birthday. It's my sixty-fifth, and those don't just come every day. So, I'd be pleased if you celebrate with me."

As Nate said this, Marchesa realized Leanne had been intently listening to her conversations with Ross and Nate. An opportunity, she thought. "Are you interested in antiques, Leanne?"

The question appeared to startle Leanne. "Maybe…"

Marchesa decided then and there to walk to Ross's antique store that day.

"I might go there today. I should begin selling some of the things I left in Ottawa. Would you care to join me, Leanne?" She had stored all the furniture and other contents of their Ottawa condo but thought it was time to dispose of things in an orderly way.

"I…no, you'll be busy…"

"Not really. I'll just give the store the details. I need to inquire what sort of arrangements are necessary to move pieces from the storage facility in Ottawa. I'm sure they do it all the time."

Marchesa explained where Ross's store was located. "It's not that far. I think I'll go after lunch. About one-thirty. If you feel like it, we could meet on the street in front of the shop. Maybe see you, then?"

"Maybe," Leanne replied, but Marchesa knew by Leanne's nervous look she wouldn't show up.

∼

Marchesa stood in front of the antique store looking into the shop through the windows. Then she quickly gazed both ways along Queen Street, not wanting to miss Leanne. Not many pedestrians. She realized a temperature in the high twenties wasn't an encouragement to walk.

Funny, I never thought I'd ever be able to convert to Celsius. I guess it's been thirty years now, and it's automatic. Occasionally, she found herself reverting to Fahrenheit. Not to check thermostat settings or the outside temperature as she did to decide what to wear for the day. That she had down. Of course, her childhood in Italy involved metric measurements, but she didn't remember a focus on temperature, maybe just distances and liquid measurements.

She'd been standing for about fifteen minutes when she realized Leanne wasn't likely to show up.

I knew she wasn't coming. Still, she was disappointed. *I don't want to force myself on her. It's just that she seems to be someone who might need to talk. Like me. I could use someone to talk with myself. She's from Boston. Maybe I'll ask her to come to a ball game with me. The Red Sox are in town again soon.*

She left the storefront, her mood for negotiation having dissipated, and walked west on Queen. But once past the Beverley

Hotel, she turned back and returned to Crown Antiques.

A young woman greeted her.

"I was speaking with Ross at the café this morning." Marchesa looked toward the office area.

"Oh, I'm sorry," the woman said. "Ross is out with a client. I'm Amanda." Amanda proffered her hand to Marchesa. "Was he expecting you? Is there anything I can help with?"

"No...no thank you. I'll just look around. Perhaps you can tell Ross that Marsha was in to see him."

"Certainly."

Marchesa wandered around the shop until she came upon a small writing desk similar to the pair she and Andy had. The one in the shop was French polished, and she knew theirs were in almost the same condition. She was surprised at the eight-thousand-dollar valuation. They'd paid nothing. Both of theirs came from Andy's family home in Glasgow. They were invaluable, but she related to them as functional and basic. Their first desks in their first flat.

8

After she left Crown Antiques, Marchesa crossed the street and headed south on John Street toward the ballpark. As she approached the Rogers Centre, she fingered the season's pass in her pocket to make sure she had it with her and wouldn't need to go home to find it. It was far too early for the seven o'clock game, so she continued past the stadium, felt and smelt the breeze coming off Lake Ontario. Between the condo towers, she had the occasional glimpse of sunlight sparkling, glittering off the water surface. *The lake*, she thought. *That's what I want. To sit on a park bench near the water.*

◊

Marchesa was intrigued by the waterfront—boardwalk, docks, green spaces with park benches. She walked past the sign directing passengers to the ferry terminal to the Toronto Islands, made a mental note to explore what possibilities the islands might have to offer. She walked on toward one of the marinas and decided she should sit awhile and relax before the game. On such a beautiful day, she was surprised none of the benches were occupied. Perhaps the heat wasn't really an inducement to walk, even along the waterfront.

Am I ready to sell my furniture? It's my history. My story. Even if I could sell it for such an obscene amount? I don't need the money. She walked toward one of the grassy areas. *I really didn't expect Leanne to show up. I'm disappointed, though. Why? Funny, that.*

She noticed a man who appeared to be watching her. He was

seated on a bench that overlooked the marina. For the second time today, she'd allowed her vigilance to lapse. When she looked again, she thought he might be one of the regulars from the café. He waved to her.

My move, she thought. Now she felt she couldn't slip away, escape. She waved back, then strolled toward his bench looking casual, or so she hoped. She wasn't certain how to greet him. *Maybe I don't remember his name.* She didn't.

"Hello," he said. "I recognize you from the restaurant. I know Ben introduced us, but you know how it is being introduced to a whole group. All that is to say, I'm George."

Nice-looking man. Neat, impeccably dressed. Perhaps a trace of an accent.

"I'm Marchesa," she replied. "I mean Marsha." *He's going to think I'm crazy. I spoke without thinking.* She paused, then smiled. "What I meant was, I thought being Marsha here would be easier than being Marchesa."

"Marchesa sounds Italian. Lots of Italians here use their Italian names."

I really don't want to talk about this.

"So, Italy?"

"A very long time ago. I left during the war," Marchesa said.

"You must have been an infant." He said that with a slightly condescending nod to an older woman.

She smiled, recognizing his attempt. "A teenager, really. But thank you."

George smiled, then continued, "I suppose you visit Italy often?"

"No, I've never been back. I know very little of Italy today."

I should have just walked by, ignored him. She stood with a non-communicative look on her face, her lips tightly closed.

"Have a seat." George patted the bench with his hand. "I know," he said. "I'm a stranger. Perhaps you don't want to talk about things like that." He looked out toward the lake. "My name is actually Jorge. I'm an immigrant. I understand. I've been here forever, but somehow it's easier to be George. I knew people would want to pronounce Jorge with a J sound. So, I picked George." He laughed.

Marchesa stared, dumbfounded.

She felt uncomfortable. She didn't know why, but she did. This was more conversation than she wished today. She looked at her watch. "Nice to talk to you, George, but I'm late. I'm meeting a friend at the Art Gallery." She was pleased how quickly she could formulate her escape.

"Maybe I'll see you at My Spot tomorrow."

Marchesa nodded. George smiled and nodded his head also. She smiled crookedly and walked away quickly. She continued without direction until she began to replay the exchange with George. She chuckled, glanced back toward the park bench. He was no longer there. *I should have been more expansive. He's probably just lonely.*

She started to think about returning to the antique store. *Must deal with my furniture. Another month's storage fees are due soon.*

Marchesa started back toward Queen Street, intent on accomplishing what she'd set out to do earlier. But as she was about halfway there, again she was overwhelmed by the sense that maybe it was too soon for closure, that she really didn't want to dispose of the contents of their home, the contents of her life with Andy. Perhaps she simply wanted a vacation from things, from responsibility. A vacation she could return from. She decided she shouldn't walk any further today if she was going to the ballgame that evening. *Or,* she thought, *maybe I won't go today. I'll just go home.*

She slowed her pace. She stopped to catch her breath after she stumbled slightly. She glared at the ground before realizing she'd tripped over nothing. She looked around. *It's all concrete. Concrete and more concrete.* Stairs to her left led to a small park. She couldn't read the sign. Maybe something else to discover, but not today. So much green space. She watched two women in some sort of interaction. The one seemed to be saying goodbye to the other. She looked at the younger of the two.

She looks a bit like Leanne. Stop it, she reprimanded herself. *That place, that restaurant place is driving me crazy. Maybe it's time to find another coffee shop.*

That George—Jorge—seems like a nice man. I should have just admitted I've kept track of things in Italy. With so much of my personal history there. Especially too, what happened to Mamma and Albertina. Tomorrow, maybe I'll talk with him. Maybe talking would help me.

Marchesa took a few steps forward in a shuffled gait. Alarmed, she stopped again. *No. Just tired. Walked too far. Need to rest.* She glanced toward the lake. *That hill was too much.* She steadied her right hand with her left. *I shouldn't get over-tired. Maybe I can sit here on the grass. Will I be able to get up again?*

She thought of Andy. Remembered when they'd visited Peterborough to see the Lift Lock. Now those were hills. It was shortly after they'd visited the Falkirk Wheel, their last trip to Scotland.

"This is the Canadian equivalent of the Falkirk Wheel. Here in Peterborough. But it's a lift lock. Does the same thing, only differently." Andy had smirked. "There are only two in North America. The other is about an hour's drive away, still on the Trent Severn waterway, near a small village called Kirkfield. Doesn't that sound so Scottish? Anyway, it was an engineering marvel for the turn of the twentieth century. The principles are the same, here and Falkirk—counterbalancing tubs of water."

"I see what you're saying," Marchesa said. "But you said while we were here you wanted to explore something else."

"It's a land formation I'd like to see. I'm sure you'll find it fascinating. It's called The Land Between. One of the best places to see the phenomenon is just north of Peterborough, around the towns of Bobcaygeon and Buckhorn."

"Why The Land Between?"

"It's a geographic and geological transition zone between the St. Lawrence lowlands, which is mainly limestone, and the Boreal Forest, which is the Canadian Shield."

"Sounds like a work journey for you."

"C'mon Marki, you'll find it fascinating too."

"How'll we get there?"

"Oh, that's your concern? Don't worry, we'll drive. We're not going to go by boat."

Marchesa and Andy laughed. Marchesa in relief.

∼

"We'll take that hiking trail," Andy said. "From what I understand, we'll be able to observe the transition along there."

As they walked along the footpath, Marchesa was glad they had grabbed their hiking poles from the car. She was becoming concerned about Andy's balance on their outings lately and was glad he had something to steady himself today.

"Look at this." Andy pointed at the smooth layer of limestone establishing a pathway ahead of them. "They call that formation limestone pavement. See how far it stretches along there? Look how flat and smooth it is. Sort of like a flattened brain."

Marchesa ignored his attempt at a joke but said, "I suspect it would be very slippery if it were raining."

"Right you are, I suppose."

They walked along the limestone until Andy stopped to point at some larger round-shaped rocks. "This looks like granite to me.

These are called erratics. They were left here by retreating glaciers in the last Ice Age. Now look at that small cliff face. That definitely looks like Canadian Shield, maybe in miniature, but you can see a transition happening."

"Thank you, Andy, I'm glad you convinced me to come."

"Oh, you are more than welcome, my love. Shall we head back home now?"

Marchesa smiled and nodded her head. Outings like this had become part of their customary weekend practice.

During the time they lived in Ottawa, they explored the whole length of the Rideau Canal, and then Andy wanted to start on the Trent-Severn waterway. When they'd travelled to the UK, they visited several of the revitalized canals. They'd become locales for Andy's two novels; his focus was on canals and waterways. Then in the last six years, Andy's sudden onset of symptoms made it more difficult to visit those canals. Now Andy was gone, most of the Trent-Severn left unvisited.

∽

"Marsha," the man said. "Are you okay?"

Marchesa felt dazed as she looked at him without recognition.

"I'm George. We were just talking down by the water."

"Yes, yes. George. Sorry. I just sat down to rest. Must have fallen asleep."

"Do you live near here?"

"Queen Victoria Gardens," Marchesa replied, then quickly added, "The retirement condos. Not the nursing home."

"Look, I'm just thinking of going back to the restaurant. Can I give you a lift?"

"Oh no, I don't want to go there."

"What I mean is can I drop you off near your place? It's on my route."

Marchesa started to say she was enjoying her walk but stopped herself. "A ride would be wonderful."

"My car's not far, just over there." George helped Marchesa to her feet. "I want to check on how Ben's doing."

Did I miss something? "What happened to Ben?"

"He may have broken his ankle."

"Really?"

"Slipped on grease or something. Richard took him for X-rays."

"I…I wasn't there this morning."

"Good thing I bumped into you then. You'll be right up to date for tomorrow morning."

Yes, she thought. *It's decided. I need to continue with the restaurant just to keep up with the people and their goings-on.*

9

This is getting to be a habit.
 Marchesa smiled as she contemplated how familiar the walk along Baldwin near the café was becoming.

Much more humid today, she thought. *A good rain should clear that out.* She was continually amazed at how easily she'd picked up the Canadian penchant for starting conversations with a weather comment. She had regarded it as a quirky provincialism when she arrived in Canada—a peculiarity of people who didn't converse easily. Her thinking about a meteorologic focus changed. She'd now experienced rapidly developing weather phenomena with violent summer and winter storms. She felt her reserve softening. Once she knew an individual, conversation became easy, humorous, intellectual. She found Canadians were more comfortable conversing with an intimate than with someone they encountered by chance.

This morning, she arrived shortly after eight. She was pleased to see her seat was available.

Perhaps it's a hierarchy thing. Something like the social behaviour of pack animals. She knew, however, that she wouldn't get into a snarling, teeth-bared confrontation just to achieve preferred seating. She had choice. She could simply leave or sit somewhere else and still enjoy an exceptional espresso. *But my seat's there, reserved for me perhaps now that I am almost a regular.*

Funny, what goes through my mind. I wonder whether others have similar thoughts. Focussing on reminiscences? Or is it an age thing?

She walked past Leanne, already seated with a cup of tea, and took *her* place. She noted Leanne had chosen a seat that would leave a gap of two chairs between them. After their confrontation about picture taking, Leanne had moved away from the window seat and now sat routinely, any day that Marchesa had been there, at the bigger table. But never beside anyone. Marchesa looked over to greet her, but Leanne continued to stare steadfastly at the liquid in her cup. She could compliment her on the dusty rose pullover and summer blouse she was wearing. Would Leanne consider that forward? Or would telling her she looked nice today be met with more than an icy stare?

A silly thought. Don't really know her, but she looks to be taking better care of herself. Not something I should say, I guess. Then before Marchesa could say anything, Ben greeted her with a smile.

"Good morning, Marsha," he said. "You'll be pleased with our pastry selection today. In fact, I thought of you when the baker showed me what was available today. *Il y a une tarte Tatin de poire.*"

"*Vraiment?*"

"*Oui c'est vrai.*" Ben seemed pleased by this exchange. His French pronunciation was decent but very Ontario, Marchesa felt.

"And I assume you'd like your usual espresso."

"Yes, Ben. Thank you very much. *La tarte aussi, s'il vous plait.*"

Something confused *les Québécois* about her French. She and Andy used to joke that she must be speaking with a Scots accent. They laughed about that.

Dear Andy. She couldn't remember who introduced them. And yet someone must have and seen them as a good fit. It didn't seem simply a chance encounter. Romance at that point in her life was confined to the novels she read when she needed a breather from the compulsory requirements of her master's program. Andy became a fixture, someone she saw around campus and nodded to in greeting. Whenever she was in the graduate students' lounge taking a rare break from studying, he was there. Coincidence, he insisted, and she believed him, and they joked about it once they were living together. She realized then how hard he worked.

Then he boldly invited her to the pub one Thursday evening. Before the war in Italy, she'd grown up with wine at home. Occasional sips at her young age. She liked it when she could have a sip and Albertina couldn't. Made her feel so grown up. Here, she'd yet to taste alcohol.

The familiarity began. Andrew became Andy. Later came the Scottish ancestry lessons.

"Aye, Andrew's my middle name. The full handle is Gregor Andrew MacGregor. Now there's a mouthful."

"Well," she replied more forthrightly than she meant, unaccustomed to the vigour of the pint of lager. "You'll be Andy to me, or I'll not be having you."

Once they were together, Andy teased her about that episode, but for a time after that pub night, Marchesa did everything she could to avoid him until she realized how much she missed seeing him.

Yes, you'd love this fine day, my Andy.

10

On her way back to her condo from the restaurant, she deviated from her normal route to walk alongside the pool and water feature in front of City Hall.

"Hello, there," a man said. Marchesa looked toward the call to see a man she thought she recognized, sitting on one of the park benches. She stood facing him for a moment, and he continued to speak. "I know you from the restaurant...from My Spot."

She was still struggling with how she knew him.

"I'm Richard. I haven't been there often lately, so you may not remember."

"I'm..." she quickly caught herself and began again. "I'm Marsha. Marsha MacGregor." She had a sudden flashback, remembering her encounter with George. It played out so similarly.

"It's good to actually meet you, Marsha. I know Ben kind of introduced us, but we've just been like ships passing...hardly in the night." He laughed. "Just ships passing. I'll stop now with that analogy."

"Nice to finally meet you, Richard. I've heard your name so often at the restaurant."

Marchesa didn't know whether to expect the conversation to develop. She now realized Richard had been at the restaurant several times when she had been there. She had assessed him as observant, always with a notebook. His laugh was infectious. Always lots of good humour at their table. *Our table*. She smiled. *Yes*, she thought, *I have taken ownership, haven't I?*

After a few more seconds, she looked at her watch and pulled the ruse that had worked with George. "I need to go, Richard. I'm meeting a friend for lunch."

"Is that someone you'll go to the ballgame with?"

That was forward, she thought. *Do I look like I'm going to the ball game?*

Marchesa had no idea how to respond. She continued her walk, continued without direction. She glanced back toward the park bench and smiled. Richard was watching her.

Is it just that I'm the new person, or are all these men lonely?

11

Next morning, Richard was quite certain the person he could see further down the street, walking in his direction, was Chantal, so he waited for her to arrive instead of entering the restaurant by himself. He knew they'd agreed to meet inside, to make it appear like they'd just bumped into each other. He wanted to protect Chantal from having to hear teasing comments that would likely be made at the table if they arrived together. In the light of day, that all appeared rather ridiculous. He would just wait for her.

"Boy, this is pretty early for me," Chantal said as she came up to Richard. "I mean, it's not that bad, but I didn't get home last night 'til almost midnight. Man, those Braves really know how to slow down a game."

"We'll just take it easy," Richard reminded her. "I looked inside. She's not here yet."

"Maybe the game was too delayed for her too. Does she come here every day?"

"I don't know if there's even a pattern. But listen, I don't want to spook her. We're not rabid paparazzi. We just want to talk — to get to know this mystery person a bit, but only if she's interested in talking." Richard deliberately held Chantal's eyes.

Richard and Chantal had agreed to meet for coffee this morning while trying to concentrate on last night's game. Chantal was right; it'd been a really slow game. Somehow, even though they were following American League rules in the Toronto park, a National League team like Atlanta still acted as if their pitcher was going to bat and practised their extra player substitutions and double switches. Really, they appropriated the game. It could have been finished easily in under three hours. It grew into a four-hour marathon. And then to have Atlanta win in the end was beyond frustrating.

During the game, Richard had told her he'd found out something about the woman.

Chantal regarded him quizzically. She still didn't know him very well, but she realized he was a kidder. Quick comeback quips for the reporters and columnists. He seemed to enjoy the repartee.

Richard told Chantal about the coffee shop he frequented, about the unforeseen appearance of Marsha several weeks ago. He admitted then that he had a funny feeling Marsha could have an interesting backstory now that Chantal had introduced the idea. No one seemed to know anything about her, yet she was so prominent to fans and sports reporters.

"Something about the way she carries herself," he said. "Her personality is such a contrast to baseball. She's refined—we're rough around the edges. We spend time analyzing every detail—she seems to look on passively, if she looks at all."

~

Richard quickly introduced Chantal to the regulars. Called her a colleague and tried to avoid having to offer any other explanation. He observed approving glances from several of the men, so he emphasized the word colleague to sidestep any wisecracks. They knew he was single, divorced for several years.

Richard and Chantal were preparing for Marsha to arrive without any real idea of how they wanted to approach her. In Richard's experience, Marsha did not seem to join into the general table banter. Once they had settled, Richard looked over to Ben and mouthed, "Marsha?"

Ben shook his head. He went to get their coffee. Ben knew that if Chantal was a journalist, her coffee order would be the same as Richard's—nothing fancy, flavourful and strong.

Richard didn't know how long they should wait. Probably after they finished their coffees, unless Marsha arrived in the meantime. It wasn't hard to put in the time. Conversation varied—sports, politics, economics—always good humoured and mostly semi-intelligent.

Eventually, as most of the others left for work, Richard turned to Chantal. "Rain delay. I guess she's not coming. Sorry to bring you on a fool's mission."

"Oh, Richard, I don't know what you intended to accomplish, but, if you'd like, I'll take your rain check."

Richard smiled. "You never know, we may be writing our way to the Dave Moore Award."

"I don't know that one."

"Elysian Fields Quarterly."

"Sure, Mister Elite Journalist, but not tomorrow. It's pretty early for me, and two days in a row no less. Award or no award."

∼

About a week, after their first attempt to encounter Marsha, Richard and Chantal met again at My Spot. This time, the Blue Jays home stand was finished, and the team was on the road for ten days.

Chantal said, "I've decided to skip the California leg, but I'll rejoin the team in Minnesota. Filing stories from California is such an exercise of diminishing returns. Once the paper has gone to bed, whatever I write only makes the next edition. Anyone with an interest either watched the game or gets the results from social media. I know you know all this, but it's stuck in my craw."

"Well, I'm skipping this set of road games. My arrangement with *The Magazine* is looser than yours. With my focus on features and opinion pieces, *The Magazine* is happy if I submit something every week."

Chantal looked around the restaurant. "You sure the woman comes here?"

"I told you she does. And when she's here, she sits at this very table."

But apparently, there was another rain delay until at least the next day.

12

The next morning, Marchesa was drinking her first espresso when she noticed Richard holding the door for a woman coming into the restaurant. Once inside, the woman turned back to look at him with a sense of familiarity. Richard steered her to the table and indicated that she should sit beside Marchesa.

Richard introduced Chantal to Marchesa as his colleague.

The three of them chatted for about half-an-hour, occasionally commenting to one of the others who joined the conversation. When Richard and Chantal got up to leave, Marchesa felt a sense of disappointment as if she suddenly realized what she'd been missing—friendly, intelligent conversation.

"I hope I'll see you again." Marchesa directed that comment to Chantal.

"Of course, I'd enjoy that."

Then Richard said, "We'd really like to talk to you about baseball some time. About your attraction to the game. But for now, duty calls. Important stuff to write about."

13

"Once we came to Canada, to Montreal, Andy, my late husband, started to become interested in baseball," Marchesa said. "He was always a football fan while we were in the UK. He even loved to get out to kick the ball around. He said it gave him something to think about other than academia."

Marchesa reached for her espresso, sipped, then smiled toward Ben in an expression of appreciation.

"He became excited about baseball. Never wanted to play himself. Liked to watch plays intricately executed with signals from coach to catcher, from base coaches to base runners, from field coach to the outfield. Andy taught me all this, the minutiae of the game."

"So, you watched the Expos?" Richard asked.

"Well, yes, he took me to Olympic Stadium several times a year."

"Had you, yourself, any experience of baseball before you came from...did you say Scotland?" Chantal asked.

"No...and yes. I did say Scotland. No to knowing anything about baseball."

"Was there something about the game specifically?"

"It was Andy's interest mainly. As I said, in the UK, it had been football, you call it soccer here, but you know what I'm trying to say."

Richard nodded his head to affirm.

"After we moved to Ottawa, he encouraged me to join him for the minor league Ottawa Lynx games. But really, by that time, I think his loyalties were shifting to the Jays. Once they established themselves and became World Series Champions, Andy's big dream was to see the great all-Canadian World Series—Montreal versus Toronto."

"Didn't we all dream that," Chantal said. "Too bad about the Expos."

"When the Expos slipped away from Montreal to Washington, Andy was ready to transfer all his attention to those Blue Jays."

"Didn't all of Canada do that?" Richard said. "That's all we had left. But didn't that generate a magnificent fan base from sea to sea and north to Iqaluit?"

"That's such an interesting account, especially with you coming from Scotland." Chantal smiled at Marchesa.

"Andy even talked whimsically about the possibility of moving to Toronto for his love of the Jays. We both could have easily found jobs and worked here. Andy was actually approached by York University."

"Did you play sports in Scotland as a child?"

"I wasn't actually born there. When I arrived there, I was almost fifteen. I was a war refugee in Europe for almost three years."

"From where?" Richard asked.

"Italy. My family was imprisoned by Mussolini for part of the war."

"Wow! So, your family left Italy because of that?" said Richard.

"We tried to leave at the end of the war, but the rest of my family didn't make it. They died on the way."

"Are you comfortable talking about that?"

"Not really." Marchesa looked around at their table and realized no one else seemed to have overheard their conversation. "Perhaps another day, another place. That just slipped out. We were talking about baseball."

14

TORONTO, JUNE 1989

When Marchesa walked into the sunroom to join Andy for cocktail hour, she sensed his excitement.

"Mike Davies—you know, Professor Mike, has two tickets for the opening ceremonies for the SkyDome in Toronto," said Andy. "It's not a sports event, but it will have spectacular entertainment with people like Oscar Peterson playing piano."

"Is Mike going?"

"No, that's what I'm trying to say. Mike gave me tickets because he can't use them. I jumped at the chance."

"When is it?" Marchesa asked.

"Day after tomorrow. Saturday."

"You expect us to go on such short notice?"

"Of course. A fantastic chance to see where the Blue Jays will be playing—their new ultra-modern stadium. The first of its kind with a retractable roof. That's so those American teams don't need to play in the snow," he added with typical Canadian deprecation.

"Will there be a game we can go to?"

"No, the Jays are playing in Boston this weekend."

"Are you suggesting we drive all the way to Toronto just for those opening ceremonies?"

"Well, I did book us train tickets for Saturday morning. We'll be in Toronto well in advance of the event. Union Station is just a few blocks from the SkyDome. And, best of all, for you, milady, I booked us a suite at the Royal York."

"Isn't that an expensive hotel?"

"The best, and, for you, it's the least I could do! We'll love it!"

She recognized his way of framing things to sell an idea. Lovingly, he formulated romantic interludes.

15

Andy was initially disappointed with their ticketed seating under the scoreboard, far away from what would eventually be home plate, but once he studied the sightlines, he felt better. "We're away from the action, but we can see the entertainment from here. I so want to see Oscar Peterson play."

"What a beautiful stadium!" Marchesa said. "I think I like it better than Olympic Stadium. Even from back here we can see the whole field very well."

"Montreal is so much closer to Ottawa, though and that's where my heart still lies," Andy said. "Go Expos!"

"I enjoyed the train trip. We could do that a couple of times a year to see a game." Then she turned her attention away and said, "Does that sound like thunder?"

"I'm not sure. The island airport is nearby, and there are sounds of boats coming from the lake. But maybe."

"Oh no, it's starting to rain." Marchesa instinctively ducked and hunched her shoulders. She didn't say anything for a few moments. "I don't feel anything, but those people in the field level seats look like they're getting wet. Look how they're pulling their tuxedo jackets over their heads."

"Now we'll see how this works! They've started to close the roof." Andy leaned forward to see beyond their seating and to watch the roof. "It's moving but very, very slowly, almost imperceptibly. I don't think that's quite as advertised."

"The performers are getting drenched, right in the middle of the gap."

"Wow! The roof sure isn't retracting very quickly!"

"Do you think we'll get to see Oscar Peterson? That beautiful piano looks to be getting pelted. Oh, those people are getting thoroughly soaked."

"Now, Glass Tiger is my true love, a rock group from just north of Toronto," Andy said. "But I think their lead singer is from Scotland. Gives a distinctively Scottish sound on their recordings."

16

TORONTO 2013

"You mentioned that your family had been imprisoned by Mussolini when we talked the other day," Richard said.

I did, didn't I? Marchesa nodded at Richard and glanced toward Chantal. *I don't know how far I want to get into this. Maybe I can take them in another direction. I don't yet know where.* She continued to nod her head slowly and pursed her lips as if trying to remember exactly what she had said.

"Well, Richard," Chantal said, "maybe it would break the ice if you tell us something of your Vietnamese heritage. Another war. Another time."

Marchesa noticed a sudden interest from around the restaurant, not only at their table, but at others as well.

"Maybe this is too public a spot for this sort of personal exchange," Marchesa said, and her voice faded.

Chantal said, "I wasn't even thinking the question could be uncomfortable or controversial. But let's find a more neutral place to talk."

∽

Consequently, for their next meeting two days later, they sat together on two benches in Nathan Phillips Square, in front of city hall. Public space for sure, but amongst a transient group of others busily coming and going.

The two journalists knew how to play for time. They sat quietly, looking around, sipping slowly on their takeout Tim Hortons coffee. Marchesa had declined their offer of coffee.

"Yes," she eventually offered, "my family was imprisoned by our own people. My father was a member of the Italian Communist Party. He was a municipal politician and became a thorn in the side of the Fascists."

"Because of my experience in Yugoslavia, I understand what you're saying," Chantal said. "Your family was imprisoned. Your parents and you? Do you have siblings?"

"Yes, a sister. So, it was my father and mother, my sister and me."

"Why your family?"

"Why us in particular or why all of us?"

"Yes, why all of you?"

Marchesa shrugged. "The fascists seemed to think communism was a disease that could infect whole families."

"That's quite a concept."

Then Richard asked, "Do you mind if I write that down?" He paused in contemplation. "I suppose no one could ever predict Mussolini."

"I visited Italy a while back," Richard said after a pause in the conversation. "My time there was far too short. There was just so much more I wanted to see. It's still on my bucket list."

"I don't know what Italy would be like today. I've never been back."

"You actually sound more English than Italian," Chantal said.

"I left Italy for good when I could. I wanted to forget."

Marchesa didn't understand her sudden compulsion to blurt out parts of her story. She'd only really talked about it with Andy. And, of course, Drago.

Richard smiled. "I understand memories," he said. "It's

something you don't always want to talk about. Especially with a journalist." He tapped his notebook once again. "I've been back to Saigon. Things are different now."

Marchesa caught that vulnerable look, did a bit of a double take, then looked away from Richard so as not to stare.

"Well," Richard said, "if you're like most other people, you're probably thinking I don't look Vietnamese."

Marchesa nodded.

"I don't explain this to many people. My father was a US serviceman."

"But you came to Canada?"

"My mother never told him about me. He shipped home before I was born. They had no more contact."

"Really? So, you're…"

"I guess you're thinking I'm a boat person, but no. My mother managed to bring me to Canada while the war was still going on."

17

TORONTO, AUGUST 1989

"Well, here we are again," Andy said as he and Marchesa walked across Front Street from Union Station to check in at the Royal York Hotel. "We'll have an early dinner before the game."

"When would you like to get to the SkyDome?"

"Certainly by six-thirty. We'll need to make our way through crowds even to get to our gate. It's sold out, so there'll be about fifty thousand people swarming around. I was lucky to get our game tickets."

∼

Once they were seated in their second level, third base-line seats, Marchesa asked Andy why he had picked St. Louis as the first game to attend in the new stadium.

"What's my favourite bird?" Andy asked.

Marchesa thought carefully before answering so she would not minimize his declaration of a favourite. "Cardinal, I guess," she said.

"And who are we playing?"

"St. Louis Cardinals."

Ah, she thought, *I should have expected Andy's typical intrigue in his rationale.*

"So, we get to watch our favourite birds duke it out—Blue Jays and Cardinals. In the wild, they are so competitive toward each other, especially around bird feeders."

"I see now," Marchesa said. "Is that a good method for picking Blue Jays opponents? That doesn't leave many teams you would be interested in, does it? I can think immediately of the Orioles and nothing else."

"You're absolutely right there. We'll need to find another reason to attend games. Remember the Canada Day game at Olympic Stadium? I'll always be up for Blue Jays playing the Expos, here or in Montreal."

"These seats are good, aren't they? There's nothing to obstruct our view of the field or the scoreboard...what do they call it? I know you told me the other day."

"It's the Jumbotron."

"Right," Marchesa said.

"You are right—the seats are great. But you know where I'd really like to sit? See home plate? Then those couple of rows of seats. They seem to be walled off from the rest of the place. And they're right behind home plate."

"Are they expensive?"

"Very, I think, and I'd guess only available as a season ticket. If you pay attention, I think you'll see they even have wait staff serving the section."

"Very impressive," Marchesa said. "But we have a great view from here."

"I'm really glad Dave Stieb is starting today. I hope he can get through seven innings and turn it over to Duane Ward and Tom Henke. We couldn't have picked a better game."

"You mean, you couldn't have picked a better game."

"Well, I suppose, Marki. Maybe I will take credit for that."

∽

The next day after breakfast, Andy and Marchesa checked out of the hotel and walked down to the Toronto harbour shoreline. As they strolled, Andy recapped the previous evening's game.

"I thought Ernie Whitt did a great job behind the plate but the highlights for me were the George Bell and Kelly Gruber homeruns. That really set the tone. The Cardinals seemed almost demoralized when the Jays ran up the score like that. Who did you like?"

"I really liked when they substituted Pat Borders for Ernie Whitt in the late innings. He played well behind the plate. Nice to see the Jays so well positioned with backups for their regulars. Augurs well for the future."

"Boy, you've got a serious interest in this game, don't you?"

Marchesa responded to Andy. "You've taught me well. Such an intellectual game in many ways. Not like when I first thought it was just bashing at balls. It was also great to watch Cito Gaston as manager. I think he'll be really good supervising the coaches and running the day-to-day operations."

"I hate to interrupt this discussion," Andy said, "but we had better head back to the station to catch our train home. Oh, wait, listen to that bird song. Look, he's high in that tree."

"He?"

"Well, yes, see that red colour. That's a male cardinal. That reminds me, I think I need to buy new bird feeders for next winter."

18

"Good morning, Marsha," Ben said.

Marchesa. Why did I ever decide to be Marsha? I'm stuck with it now. No longer Marchesa. She wondered whether she'd said it aloud when she saw Ben's puzzled face. She missed the rest of what he said, focussed as she was in her thoughts. *Why am I hiding?*

"This is a country of immigrants," Andy had told her. "People may stumble over your name at first, but they'll ask how to pronounce it and what it means. You know, they'll want to know its derivation. Here they are interested in knowing more about other cultures."

Marchesa found that to be true in Montreal and Ottawa. She wasn't sure yet about Toronto, although Andy claimed it was probably the most cosmopolitan city in the world.

"Just a sprain," Ben said again. "Thank goodness."

"Sorry, Ben. I meant to ask how you were. But somehow, I'm lost in my thoughts. I guess you could say last night's storm spooked me." Marchesa thought Ben looked none the worse for wear. She'd worried about him after her conversation with George.

She often tried to insert idioms into her conversation. Not jargon so much but expressive words. She was fascinated by the flexibility of the English language. Yet, at the same time, she mourned the complete disintegration of grammatical construction and knew it would not bode well for modern communication. In fact, while she believed taking liberties and inventing euphemisms was the way language would continue to evolve, it was her belief that a high proportion of today's youth was functionally illiterate.

"I'm afraid we can't make espresso this morning because of the power outages," Ben continued. "We can serve coffee, though, because we made lots earlier." He motioned toward the phalanx of large stainless steel carafes standing ready on the counter. "When the power's steady again, I'll turn the espresso maker back on."

"Then, may I please have a large, strong black...what blend have you made?"

"We combined beans from Kenya, Columbia, and Sumatra. Our own blend. Full flavoured but low acid."

"Then that's exactly what I'd like, please."

As Ben left to fill her order, Sally approached quietly even though she was not serving that table today.

"How are you this morning, Marsha?" she asked. "George told me you were feeling a little weak the other day. This is the first chance I've had to talk with you since then."

"I'm fine, thank you, Sally."

"I'm glad to see you. I'm a little surprised you made it with the rain and all."

"It's becoming so much part of my morning routine. When the storm eased off, I thought I'd come along." Marchesa smiled. "And I have my umbrella."

"Glad you're here."

"Me too," Marchesa said as she turned back to the table.

Before Ben could return with coffee, a bolt of lightning discharged alongside a reverberating bellow of thunder. The window in the door to the street shattered. Glass shards exploded into the room. Lightning continued to flare. Ear-splitting thunder persisted with a rolling boom, seemingly unending. Marchesa was anxious, but she was not a screamer. It had served her life well to control her urge to panic. Calm in the eye of the storm. Her ears hurt. Blood pounded in her head. The tremor in her right hand was suddenly uncontrollable. She pulled her arm into her body for support, but the shake did not subside. That amplified her disquiet.

The customers stood, gawking at the pulverised door.

"Everyone behind the counter," Ben said with authority. "Everyone! Please! Quick!"

Marchesa moved as quickly as her body could respond. She thought maybe a tree branch had crashed through the window. *Where would that have come from? I don't remember any trees on this part of the street.*

"Marsha, let me help you." Sally placed her arm on her shoulder to guide her behind the bar with the others. Marchesa recognized most of the regulars along with three or four strangers.

Rain roared outside as they waited behind the protection of the counter in hushed, almost reverent silence. Marchesa realized that Sally, like Drago, was concerned about her. About her well-being. *My second guardian angel. No, my third. Andy was my second.*

19

ORKNEY 1956

"Let's move along to that fishing shelter." Andy touched her shoulder and pointed toward what she saw as a mound of stones along the shore. No matter how hard she tried, she could hardly follow his line of sight through the horizontal Orkney rain driven ahead of the wind. When they'd left the village of Evie to hike the shoreline to the Broch of Gurness, the sky was overcast, but the cloud cover was breaking up, promising a fine day ahead, at least as fine as an Orkney day could be in May. Their plan was simple, to look across to the island of Rousay, then return to Evie in time for dinner at the guest house.

"I want to look across to the island," Andy said. "I've never been over on Rousay but I will need to come back as part of my research. It's such a treasure trove of geography and archeology from the Viking and Pictish inhabitants. Now there's a study for an economic geographer. The Picts were a very early example of establishing the roots of an economy."

Marchesa was surprised to hear about Andy's research interests. They had never discussed these aspects of his personality in the short time they had known each other. Andy had proposed this excursion only two days previously, and yet here they were, neither having had much time to think about it.

"You must see, nay, experience, Orkney," he had said. "Else you will continue to have great gaps in your knowledge of Scotland.

You've got to feel Scotland."

Before she could ask about lodging, he said, "I've arranged for us to stay at a guest house in Evie. Oh, you'll love the wee village, the fishing docks and the Iron Age ruins of the Broch of Gurness."

"Ruins," she said. "I've seen plenty of ruins."

"Ach, but these are historic. Maybe three thousand years old. They call it the Egypt of the North because of the treasure trove of ruins and relics."

Unlike ruined Europe, she thought but simply nodded. "Oh, of course."

"Rousay belonged to the Norse until they ceded it to Scotland around the same time as Christopher Columbus was headed across the Atlantic Ocean to supposedly discover America."

They had talked of going off to see more of Scotland. Marchesa was such a serious student, she hadn't even seen much of Edinburgh outside the university. When they arrived at the guest house, Marchesa realized that Andy had arranged for them each to have their own room. Marchesa had not asked him about his plans, but she knew she was right to trust Andy.

Now, the rain came in from the North Sea so fast it caught them totally unprepared. The wind velocity increased rapidly and transformed a horizontal squall into a torrential deluge. They staggered carefully across and around the sea-worn boulders, wrapping arms about each other's waists, pressing together for support, fighting the elements to maintain balance. Eventually, they reached the stone hut, a structure formed from those very boulders with an open doorway facing away from the prevailing weather. They ducked into the subterranean bothy. Suddenly, the deafening howl and brutal slashing of gale force winds magically quieted. No need to continue to press with all bodily force to counteract the tyrannical storm.

Andy showed Marchesa the charcoal remains of earlier fires and told her that the small opening high in the back wall served as a chimney.

"These shelters were used by fishermen to escape storms. They would pull their boats high up onto the rocks, safe from the crashing waves. You can still see where vees were set into the beach stone, punctuating with protected inlets along the vast shorelines of the Orkney Islands and beyond. Now you know how fast the weather can change."

Andy guided her to sit on the rock benches. "Norwegian fishermen were probably the first to seek refuge here. That would be back about the time of the Picts. They fished here and settled these islands long before there was a Scotland."

Some kind soul, a previous shelter seeker, had left a small pile of driftwood kindling, dried peat, soft grasses, and thistle down as fire-starter material.

That must be the expectation, she thought. *Replace what was used for the subsistence of the next shelter seekers.*

The temperature dropped quickly with the rain. Marchesa and Andy were soaked. He set about to start the fire. She was impressed with his ability. He'd done this before, this hiking and making do with primitive conditions. She'd done forced hikes and lived in less than desirable conditions. But this journey was of their own free will, an expedition to discover part of northern Scotland. They had only met a few weeks prior, but it felt so natural for Marchesa to spend time with this man.

Once the fire began to drive the dampness from the hut, Andy encouraged her to remove her wet outer layers, her jacket, sweater, and skirt. He held her close to warm her shaking body. His body pressed into hers with gentle, caring force, not the force of nature. She didn't know whether she was trembling from cold or excitement. When Andy asked if she would like to make love with him, she said yes without hesitation. That was exactly what she wanted. Then, gently, he removed her underclothing.

He admired her body with his hands until he eventually touched her in places she'd never been touched. Then he lay on the stony floor and eased her down on top of him before gently entering her. They made love for the first time. That, too, of their own freewill.

As he held her later, she allowed herself to relax completely in his arms.

20

TORONTO 2013

Marchesa herself couldn't see out to the street, but one of the voices in the dim café said the driving rain reminded him of the 2004 flood.

"That was 2005, actually," Ben said. "I know because I had just taken over the restaurant, and here I was, already faced with fixing the damage from over six inches of rain."

"Okay, I stand corrected. 2004, 2005. A while ago."

Marchesa realized it had been Simon speaking. But with the window broken, the din was horrifying, intimidating. *I want to hide. I want to be with friends. I want to be with Andy.*

"Spadina's a river. Baldwin's a tributary," another man, one of the strangers, exclaimed.

"Yeah, that's right," Ben spoke above the noise. "Simon, you might get to use your kayak."

"No, I'm just going to stay here and drink coffee." Simon smiled. "Maybe you'll bring some wine up from the basement. Special circumstances, eh Ben? Like you did for the World Cup."

Marchesa watched Ben's response. He simply smiled and shrugged.

Such a nice man, Marchesa thought. *Grace under pressure.*

She glanced around. *Leanne's not here. I didn't see her leave. Maybe she finally gave up on the tea. Just not prepared to her exacting standard.*

She looked composed earlier. Not so agitated. Maybe she's made peace with herself.

I don't have my coffee yet. Isn't that silly? Measuring restaurant service levels during emergencies. Like a surprise exam. Pop quiz, the students call it. Give me an essay on normative flood containment practices while continuing a high level of customer service in specialty coffee shops.

She looked at the regulars. She'd been so preoccupied with herself this morning, with her reflections. Visions, memories, reminders. Messages. Perhaps prompts. *I hadn't thought of that 'til now. I've missed something.* She watched the others at her table. *Charlene is dressed so casually. She's talking with the younger woman — the one she never has the time of day for. David, that nice man, helping Charlene keep her balance. She must have been injured. Nice people. I'm the trespasser, intruding on their morning routine, the kibitzing chatter, my relationship with Ben and Sally, maybe Richard. It's taken weeks, but they're drawing me into their circle.*

I like it here. Sally rescued me. Ben makes me feel like more than a customer. I'll sell the furniture. Maybe Sally would go with me to Crown Antiques... Leanne's not here. I hope she's okay.

Still no electricity, but the furious crash of the storm had abated. Marchesa realized that this Simon person was helping Ben screw plywood sheeting over both the broken window and the intact one as reinforcement. That reduced the noise to the point where she was able to concentrate on her own thoughts again. *It's so dark without the window light. Who lit the candles? It is pleasant here. I can't... weak... must sit down.*

Marchesa slid slowly to the floor.

21

EDINBURGH 1956

"Then what will you be? I mean, will you be a geographer or an economist?"

"Yes, exactly."

Marchesa looked confused, her usual reaction to Andy's obtuse responses.

Andy was explaining to Marchesa that once he defended his thesis at the University of Edinburgh for his PhD in Geography, he expected to go on to Oxford for another doctorate in Economics. "Really, it's a very new field. Well, I'm not certain it actually is a field quite yet. We're calling it economic geography. It's the study of people earning their living in different geographic regions. We would look at how systems vary by area and focus on interrelations and linkages."

"Sounds complex. But where will you work?"

"I may need to go to the colonies." Andy laughed.

"Where?"

"Canada, most likely. Although maybe Australia. There is some research being done to determine whether human activities could possibly have some effect on climate. Some parts of Canada have relatively untouched regions of arboreal forest that could be studied."

Marchesa looked shocked, hoped her disappointment didn't show.

Andy picked up on her concern. "I hope you would want to come with me. I mean, to Oxford, and after that, maybe Canada."

Marchesa remained silent. *So much moving around*, she thought.

22

TORONTO 2013

"Marsha, Marsha. Can you hear me?" Ben moved to comfort her.

Andy...

"Let's clear some space." Ben's words floated around Marchesa. "Sally, grab that blanket from the office. And something for her head...one of those small bench cushions."

Andy... it's still raining... will we stay all night? I love you.

Marchesa opened her eyes and smiled brightly. She wasn't aware of the slight drooping of her lips on the left and a twist on her right side.

"Call 9-1-1, Sally. We need an ambulance," Ben said.

Oh, don't go to that bother. There's no pain. I'm...I'm...

"It may be some time before they come," Sally spoke quietly to Ben. "All emergency vehicles are in use."

That's okay, dear. I'll just rest here, Andy. I just want to stay home. No machines, Andy, you promised. Like we did for you...Don't let them...don't let them hook me to machines, my dear. You promised, Andy...Andy, amore mio...

23

OTTAWA 2011

"How was your appointment?" Marchesa asked.

"Fine." Andy looked down averting eye contact. Then he raised his head. "No, it wasn't fine." He paused then said, "I don't want to live like that." He reached toward her.

She took his hand into her two. She suddenly didn't know what to say. She knew his prognosis was probably not good. But he had only just received his diagnosis. He was healthy now. That was what mattered most…keeping him healthy, whatever it took. She couldn't imagine herself without him.

"Marki, I have done the things I love all my life. I can't imagine living if I can't travel, can't hike and canoe, ski, and golf…"

"But we all slow down as we age. We do different things or the same things differently."

"That's my Marki. All her ethical mumbo-jumbo platitudes."

They both laughed. Some of the bioethical issues Marchesa studied and recommended in her work gave him no end of amusement. She, for her part, good-naturedly accepted his teasing. "Chief parking lot attendant," he would joke about one of the original problems referred to her in her hospital consult. It was simple, she'd decided; patients needed to park closer to the ER entrance than the doctors and hospital staff. That proposal had not gone over well with any of the interested parties.

"But seriously Marki. I can't imagine the frustration of trying to do anything, anything, when I'm strapped to an oxygen tank."

"We need to accept our limitations."

"Do we, now? For God's sake, Marki, I'm eighty years old." And he knew he had never admitted to having limitations.

"Eighty-two."

"My point is, I've had a good life."

"What is it *you* want, Andy?"

"I don't know exactly, but I expect I'll know when I've suffered enough."

"But you're not suffering."

"No. Not now. And I don't want to."

∼

They both had anticipated Andy's first visit to the pulmonary fibrosis clinic. She suggested she could accompany him, but Andy refused her offer. She supposed he didn't wish to be defined as ill enough to require a companion caregiver. He went alone. Now, he conveyed his thoughts about the information session held in a small lecture theatre at the hospital.

"How many people were there?" Marchesa asked.

"I'd guess about thirty participants and five hospital staff." He explained how he thought he was probably one of the oldest. And probably the healthiest. "The staff were quite good. Lots of experience, I suspect. And, at least, they didn't call us clients. You know what bothers me most? I'd bet almost half the people there were personal care workers for poor wretches like me if I let that happen. Those outpatients, living at home, strapped into wheelchairs, disguised with oxygen masks, tanks strapped to the chairs. I'd hate to see what the hospitalized patients look like. I don't want anything to do with this."

∼

The next day, Andy sat with Marchesa in their sunroom, always a favourite spot for a cup of tea. Even in their condo, the large windows gave an unexpected sense of privacy, allowing autumn sunshine to enter their home without exposing them to a feeling of vulnerability, never a focus for their neighbours as close as they all were in this housing development.

"I need a plan," Andy said. "And I will need your help." He raised his hands to silence her objections. He explained that he just wanted to talk out loud about the ideas he had buzzing in his brain since his appointment.

"Oh, Andy, I've been thinking about things." In fact, she'd thought of little else since he came home from the clinic the day before. "I think I know what you want me to do. That terrifies me."

"I don't want you to put your life in jeopardy, Marki. I'm not asking you that. But to do it myself…Damn it! Let's stop skirting the issue! Talking in euphemisms!"

"It's okay."

"No, it's not okay. I'm talking about killing myself." He turned in his chair to look directly at her. "I want to stay with you as long as possible. I hope you know that. But if I push it too far, it means I may not be competent when the time comes."

"Have you lost hope?" Marchesa's face mirrored her distress.

"No. I want there to be a cure. I hope for a cure. If I were religious, I'd pray for a cure. Something amazing, miraculous. Something ground-breaking just around the corner. Banking on that likelihood is so wishful. If nothing transpires, I don't want to live as a vegetable. You know, the clinic yesterday…seeing those people not just dependent but coupled to their wheelchairs, fighting for each breath while in obvious pain, requiring an attendant to look after every need. That's not me."

"I'm here to help."

"Believe me, I'll know when enough is enough. No, I don't want to die prematurely. I think I will know when I've had enough. But I may not be capable then. I'm worried that I probably won't qualify for medically assisted death whenever that proposed legislation finally comes into play. My death may not be imminent enough for that. And I don't want to travel somewhere else, get into somebody else's bureaucratic line-up, just to die."

Marchesa got out of her chair, knelt beside Andy. "I hear what you're saying, my love," she said.

~

It's not as if they hadn't discussed medically assisted dying before now. In fact, Marchesa had introduced the *assisted dying* terminology rather than *assisted suicide* to Andy.

"Most ethicists prefer *dying* to *suicide*, but it's far from a universal sentiment," she had said.

"What's the difference?" Andy asked. "Surely, medical assistance is the key point. Otherwise dying is simply that. Dying."

"Oh, but it's the stigma attached to suicide. As ethicists we try to remove humiliation and potential disgrace from what is destined to become a medical procedure in the near future. I know to you it may be just jargon."

"No, I get it. I understand what you mean."

Andy poured them both another cup of tea with no idea how soon he would wish to return to discussing this subject.

24

TORONTO 2013

Richard walked toward the fifth-floor solarium of Toronto General Hospital. He and Chantal agreed to meet there that morning so they could each visit Marchesa in the ICU. Then they would walk to the ballpark in plenty of time before the afternoon game.

Richard always remembered the criticism of the stadium being built downtown, the yet unnamed domed edifice so close to the lake when there was so much vacant space available north of the city. He had joined that criticism. He had argued in his column that subway construction would also be sped up to the dual advantage of a now retro Toronto unprepared to be a world-class city. Would attendance at the games be anything like it was nowadays with sell-out crowds? He had his doubts. Now he'd done an about face. There was something progressive about having sporting facilities, theatres, and other entertainment facilities right downtown; public transit readily available, easy walking distance within the business districts and shopping quarters. That's how it would be for him this morning from the Discovery District and its concentration of hospitals and research facilities on University Avenue.

When he reached the solarium, Chantal wasn't there, so he sat in one of the more comfortable chairs. He knew she would show up; she'd probably just been waylaid by work or traffic. He suddenly realized he didn't even know where Chantal lived. That wasn't something they'd talked about. Their focus had just been baseball until it switched to Marchesa.

When Chantal and Richard had last discussed Marsha, Chantal said, "I like her. There's something about her life. But, you know, she's holding back. Something just under the surface."

Richard simply nodded in agreement, so Chantal continued to talk. "My initial interest was simply getting to know about the lady, just so she doesn't remain a complete mystery to me."

She had Richard's attention, but he still wasn't saying anything. "But there's more to it," she continued. "I'm convinced about that. Maybe we can take a different tack."

"You may be right," Richard said. "Maybe if we ask questions about her career, assuming she had one. Or about her husband and his career, also assuming he had one. We seem to have reached an impasse in discussing much more about Italy. Mind you, I admit she has shared some pretty interesting things. Maybe we can find a way to get on to something else."

Richard continued to sit, waiting for Chantal to show up, but now looking at his watch, he realized the available time was running out. He had arranged to interview Pete Walker, the Blue Jays pitching coach, before the game. He considered that Chantal had expressed some reluctance to visit Marchesa in hospital.

"It's not like I really know her."

"She seems to have taken a shine to you, though."

"Yeah, I guess." Chantal had shrugged and agreed to join him there in the morning.

∽

"Richard." A tall man in a suit approached him. Richard realized he'd been sitting at the back of the solarium. As he approached, Richard recognized him and jumped up to shake his hand.

Richard smiled. "Inspector," he said. "Is this a stake-out, Dave?"

Dave snorted and clapped Richard on the shoulder. "How you doin', buddy?" Then Dave winked and tilted his head slightly. Dave was acting in character.

"You got someone in here?"

"Yeah, a woman we've come to know because of the Blue Jays."

"New love interest?"

"No, no. You're a baseball fan. Maybe you've seen her in the stands when you watch the home games on TV."

"Are you talking about the one they're calling Home Plate Lady?"

"Probably...Mar..."

"No names." Dave raised his palms toward Richard to signal him not to say anything. Dave looked around the room to ensure he was unobserved. "We know who she is. I didn't realize she was a patient here."

"You know who she is? What are you talking about?"

"Check her out with your Ottawa contacts. Unofficially. About her husband's death. They were puzzling over a possible assisted suicide. I don't think she's still under investigation, but she was a person of interest."

Richard couldn't supress his look of surprise.

"Is she the reason you're here, Dave?"

"No, no. Like I said, I didn't know she was here. But, as you know, this conversation never happened." Dave resumed his role. "Glad to see you, buddy. We need to have a drink." He was talking loudly as he walked away.

Richard knew Dave as a teetotaller.

∼

Richard realized that Chantal had arrived in the solarium and had observed Dave walking away while still talking to him.

"A friend?" she asked.

"Oh, from way back. High school, actually. In Vancouver."

"Every time I'm with you, you seem to meet someone you know."

"Yeah," Richard agreed. "It's not really such a big town. Everyone I know, from Vancouver, from Edmonton, from Ottawa, seems to eventually end up in Toronto." He decided he wouldn't discuss Dave's cryptic message with her until he'd had time to investigate its meaning.

∼

"Dehydration," Marchesa said. "That's all it was. Heart strong, blood pressure good."

Richard stood back from the bed so Chantal could move closer.

"They'll move me to a medical ward for a few days before I go home. They're concerned that I live alone even though I told them nursing care can be arranged."

Chantal nodded her head in agreement with Marchesa, who continued, "Dehydration is very strange for me. I worked in the medical system for so long. Everyone used to carry a water bottle with them."

Richard picked up the work reference and smiled with satisfaction. "I assume you're not working still?"

"Oh no, I'm retired. Except when I'm called upon by the government or some organization to sit on a panel."

"What was your field?"

"Bioethics."

"Really?"

"Oh yes, but that's not normally a conversation starter." Marchesa laughed quietly.

∼

"She's talking quickly. Almost falling all over herself to get her words out." Chantal looked toward Richard once they left the ICU and were in the corridor. "Almost like stream of consciousness."

"Well, I still don't know her much better than you do, but I agree. That's more information in one go than from all our other conversations."

25

Richard had maintained his newspaper contacts in Ottawa even though they were not useful for his current baseball columnist job. Several remained good friends. They'd get together for a ski week in Quebec almost every winter. Two of them had cottages where they'd have one or two fishing weekends in the summer. Richard retained his interest in the ins and outs of politics. He was mostly glad it was no longer his beat. As a matter of fact, he usually managed to write his political columns as sports allegories, drawing in the Ottawa Senators or the Ottawa Lynx when there was still a baseball farm team there.

Hank Barton at the *Ottawa Citizen* was always reliable, not given to gossip. Richard asked him to run the name Marsha MacGregor through the archives. Then he remembered someone at the restaurant — Jorge, he thought, had said something that sounded like *Marchesa* to refer to Marsha one day. Richard asked Hank to search Marchesa as well just in case there was a hit.

Hank came up with Andrew MacGregor and Gregor A. MacGregor. Then, from the death notice, he uncovered that Professor Andrew MacGregor's wife was Marchesa di Mentone.

There had been a few stories about MacGregor's death. Police contacts told Hank that MacGregor's wife was a person of interest in what looked like an assisted suicide, but the investigation led to no more evidence or charges. Hank recalled that when he originally read the account, he had decided not to write anything speculative about the professor's death and aborted his research.

When they were talking, Hank asked Richard to keep him

apprised of the situation, especially if he decided to pursue a story angle. Richard's questions piqued his interest once again.

26

OTTAWA 2011

Andy had just mentioned DNA testing out of the blue one day. He asked about Marchesa's opinion from an ethicist's point of view.

"I'm not sure what to think yet. This ability to be tested individually, seemingly at will, is so new."

"Surely, it would be a topic of conversation amongst your colleagues?"

"Oh, you're certainly correct about that. We discussed it frequently. And I'm sure they're discussing it today," said Marchesa. "So far, we restrict ourselves to looking at medical use. I guess in the vernacular, it's considered a game changer, but medical use is where our priorities belong. DNA analysis can show a genetic predisposition for certain diseases like Huntington's chorea. The ethical question is, should that information be shared with patients? More frightening, do those predictions become part of one's medical history? As such, should that be shared along with current medical history? Life insurance companies would love that, especially in countries like the US."

"And, the problem is..."

"Standard medical history indicates high blood pressure. It does not predict pulmonary fibrosis."

"What about cancer genes like the breast cancer tumour markers?"

"Okay. The question is, what do physicians or patients do with the results?"

"Well, as you know, I have pulmonary fibrosis. The diagnosis has been made," Andy said. "So, there would be no benefit to me determining whether I have a disposition toward the disease. But it could be advantageous if we had had kids. Would they be predisposed? Would they want to know? With abortion now available, would we have wanted to know?"

"You've discovered the ethical problem," Marchesa said. "My perspective has always been not to let the humanity get lost in numbers and data points. People, especially in health care, live lives with families and friends. Statistics is merely a tool."

"Whoa, that's heavy lifting. I'm certainly relieved you're retired. I can't imagine sitting around all day pondering things like this."

"You seem to think it makes good conversation, though."

Andy laughed and shrugged his shoulders. "Maybe," he said.

"Maybe that's why I still go to the office once a week."

∼

A few days later, a parcel arrived in the mail addressed to Marchesa. When she opened the mystery package, it contained two boxes labelled *FindYourOriginsDNA*. When she read the insert, she realized she'd received consumer test kits.

"Oh, they've arrived," Andy said when he came home. "That was fast." When he appeared to read a level of concern in Marchesa's body language, he said, "They had a sale. I just bought them on a lark."

Marchesa knew Andy did nothing on a whim, only after careful research, even when he shopped for clothing.

"I thought it might be fun to search out our roots," he said. "I might be a Viking. Just imagine."

Marchesa smiled. Whatever her concerns, she always appreciated Andy's ability to lessen the tension with a light-hearted reaction. She had a sudden memory of something Drago had said so many years before. *Hardly years*, she thought, *decades*. She couldn't remember the context or his exact words but a suggestion that her family might have come from Yugoslavia. Something else about her name coming from Edgar Allan Poe. She certainly knew who Poe was now but had never understood the Yugoslav reference. After a long, almost agonizing discussion, she realized she could submit the test but didn't need to pay attention to any of the results. *I might as well learn what's involved*, she thought. *See any obvious pitfalls. Purely research.* Just examining the kit gave her the sense that the results could not possibly have legal standing.

∽

Andy couldn't stop talking about his likely heritage once he received his results. "Just think," he would say. "Sixty-seven percent Irish-Scottish. Aye, that'd be short on the Irish except for the wee bit of Celtic. I prefer the homeland designation."

"Show me what the report's like," Marchesa said. "What's the rest of your genetic makeup?"

"Oh, you know, those English managed to slip in for some thirty percent. But maybe it's only the way FindYourOrigins expresses it as a conglomerate — England, Wales, Northwestern Europe."

"That's pretty broad, isn't it?"

"Well, England was formed of the Saxons and the French back then. Actually," Andy continued, "I wouldn't mind if my genes were partly Welsh." He paused then, and with a bit of a smile, he carried on. "But the interesting thing is, five percent Scandinavian."

"Scandinavian?"

"Yes, so much of northern Scotland was actually settled by the

Norse. Remember when we visited Orkney…That's it! I knew I was part Viking."

"How could I forget that? We sealed our fates that weekend, that magical exploration."

Andy smiled, then carried on. "Anyway, so much of Orkney has a history with Scandinavian fishermen. Sorry Marki…Scandinavian fishers is what I meant to say."

Marchesa appreciated his sensitivity to her gender neutral preferences. They joked at first, but then he was careful to use the term *woman* instead of *lady*, for example. A woman is a woman she told him, not defined narrowly on an assumption of social standing.

After a while, he asked if she had submitted her saliva sample.

"You must realize I haven't been that interested. But after seeing your results, I'm feeling a bit of excitement. My main concern is that the analysis depends on a significant number of observations. You know, statistically. For legitimate results, there needs to have been a large number of people interested or affluent enough to submit their samples." She thought again of Drago's long-ago comment about a Yugoslav connection. How many individuals from former Yugoslavia would have participated in DNA testing? She should make the effort to find out what she could, although she certainly was not expecting anything, since her immediate family was dead.

27

TORONTO 2013

My Spot restaurant had been closed for essential repairs for almost three weeks following the storm. Richard was there the morning of the reopening. Nothing flashy or official, but he was pleased to see the restaurant restored and redecorated. His thoughts were with Marchesa, wondering if she would come back or whether she would remain traumatized from her experience. He had visited her in hospital a second time, but the third time, when he went with Chantal, Marchesa had been discharged. He fought the notion of his visits being journalistically predatorial. He really had become captivated by her regal demeanour. The mystery persisted. What made a woman who was so reserved an adamant baseball presence? What made Queen Elizabeth passionate about the Queen's Plate? When would she let her hair down?

"Do you know how to get in touch with her?" Chantal asked.

"Not really," Richard said, then continued, "Actually, I have no idea. I think she lives in one of the condos near the Harbour Castle Hotel, but I don't know which one."

"How did she seem last time?"

"Pretty good. I don't really know physically. We walked around the corridors, but she needed one of those three-pronged canes for balance. She was in good spirits."

Richard really didn't expect Marchesa today. Not many of the regulars showed up, so he bantered with Ben.

As Richard was getting ready to leave, there she was.

"Marsha," Richard smiled as he greeted her, "how nice to see you."

Marchesa smiled back but said nothing immediately.

Richard motioned toward her usual seat, inviting her to join him. "Nobody here today. I could use your company."

Marchesa looked around and nodded her head in affirmation, as if she were approving the repairs.

There were so many things Richard wanted to discuss, but he didn't know how to start, how not to seem too intense, how not to turn Marsha off from talking to them. He didn't know whether he should wait until he and Chantal were together.

"So, how do you assess your hospital experience now that you're back to civilization?"

Marchesa directed a quizzical look at Richard, then paused as if she were seriously considering his question and formulating an answer. "Actually," she said with a grin, "it was all very civilized. I think I was treated very well. Everyone was very patient." She raised her eyebrows as she looked at Richard. "No, really," she continued, "everyone was very professional. But it was my first experience with a Canadian hospital. That is," she stammered slightly, "as a patient. Of course, I worked in hospitals."

"You would be used to dealing with medical professionals."

"Yes, of course."

"Since you worked in the Ottawa hospital system, you realize your treatment there would have been as good as here in Toronto."

"Yes, and I like to think even better." Marchesa smiled a knowing smile.

I worked Ottawa into it, Richard thought. *Can I make the jump to finding out why she left Ottawa? Was it her husband's death?*

Marchesa moved on. "My final diagnosis was dehydration. My electrolytes were all askew. That whole storm experience didn't help either. I need to eat properly, drink more fluids. I can certainly get enough exercise if I continue my walking."

"Does that mean you would stop coming here?"

"Oh no, I'm quite attached to the place. And it has probably provided the most proper meals I've been eating lately. If anything, I should come here more frequently, not just twice a week."

"I, for one, would welcome seeing you more often."

"I have started to have some meals in the dining room at Queen Victoria Gardens, and I try to make some more decent dinners myself."

"That's hard, cooking for one."

"Andy used to make most of our meals at home. He had the patience to make even the most basic meal seem gourmet."

"Sounds like you miss him a lot."

"Yes, Richard, that would be an understatement. You know, I have the impression you want to ask me something, but you don't quite know how I'll respond or react."

"No, not exactly … well, yes. I wonder why you left Ottawa. You seem to have loved living there."

"That's it?" Marchesa looked away from Richard and gripped her coffee mug.

"Yeah, that's it. Why Toronto? You sound like you really enjoyed Ottawa and Montreal."

28

Marchesa thought about Richard's questions frequently during the few days since they talked at the restaurant. *Does he have a reason for asking?* she wondered. *He is a reporter after all.*

She was pleased to see Chantal sitting beside Richard at the table when she arrived at My Spot this morning. *They make a good couple*, she thought. *Wonder what the age difference is?*

She greeted the regulars and appreciated that they asked after her health and seemed genuine with their concern.

"It's great to see you back," Richard said, then chuckled and added, "What I really meant is it's great to be back. I've missed the place. But more to the point, I've missed all of you. And Ben of course!"

From the way Richard was glancing around, Marchesa couldn't really be positive whether he was aiming his comment at her, Chantal, or the rest of the table. He wasn't talking loudly enough to be directing it at everyone, so she decided she or Chantal were his focus.

Chantal shrugged. "I certainly like the place even though it's only maybe my fourth or fifth visit."

Richard said, "Need to leave soon. I'm interviewing Audisio before the game. He's been a great acquisition for Boston."

"Do you know of him at all, Marsha?" Chantal asked. "He's Italian. Not usual for an MLB player."

"I really don't know anything of those few European players. There aren't many of them," Marchesa stated. "And after all, I left Italy almost seventy years ago."

29

Chantal watched Richard as he excused himself from the table, having explained to the regulars that he had pre-game interviews scheduled. They dismissed him with good natured ribbing. Chantal wasn't ready to leave, so she stayed seated when he got up and walked toward the door.

Chantal saw a great opportunity to talk alone with Marchesa. She felt Marchesa seemed pleased she stayed behind.

Then, almost immediately, Ross, who she recognized as the antiques dealer, moved to take Richard's vacated seat.

Ross directed his comments to Chantal. "Ever since you first came here with Richard, I had the feeling that I knew you somehow. That I recognized you," Ross said. "I often read your articles about the Jays, but it was something else."

"Like what?"

"Well, for instance, I thought I recognized Marsha when she first came here, but I didn't know from where. Sounds like I have an attention deficit, doesn't it? I thought probably from her being in my antique store, but that wasn't it," Ross explained. "It took quite a long while before I realized it was her TV image on the Jays games."

Marchesa felt herself cringe at that sort of recognition.

"And with me?" Chantal asked.

"I think it's Collingwood. Blue Mountain. Going back into ancient history, there was a fifteen-year-old downhill racer who was tearing up the circuit. Chantal Jefferson. Would that have been you?"

"I, um…"

"Sorry, I know we were introduced by Richard along with the rest of the table gang. I'm Ross."

"Well, Ross, thank you for asking. That's quite a memory you have. Yes, that was me about twenty-five years ago."

"That memory is with me, but I've lost track since. I remember reading your Olympic Games reports and wondering whether you were possibly the same person…the downhill racer. Did you do more competitive skiing beyond junior?"

"I kept at it for about ten years. Never quite made the national team, but was always there on the cusp."

"Did you race internationally?"

"For sure," Chantal said. "I kept up the training and raced the big courses. Always ready, but always on the B team."

"Did you get tired of it all?"

"A lot of travel, not much personal time. In the end, though, I wasn't getting the financial support the team members got, so I needed to consider a career off the slopes."

"What did you do about it?"

Boy, she thought, *Ross is just so full of questions.*

"While I was still racing, I studied journalism parttime. I thought I'd better get moving toward a real career, so I started back at Carleton fulltime."

Chantal glanced back to where Marchesa had been sitting and suddenly realized she had missed her opportunity to talk with her without Richard directing the conversation. Marchesa must have slipped away while Ross was interrogating her.

Ross adjusted his chair, pulling it closer into the table. With both elbows on the table, he leaned in closer to Chantal.

"Are you and Richard, you know…?"

Chantal was startled by the question, and she wasn't totally certain what he was asking. Did he want to know if they were in a relationship, or was it about their level of intimacy? She simply shook her head and said, "No!"

"Sorry," Ross said. "I was just wondering. I think some of the others were too."

"Please do not report back to the table." Chantal smiled at Ross.

30

OTTAWA 2011

Andy seemed annoyed that Marchesa wasn't more excited about having her *FindYourOriginsDNA* testing done. He was obviously pleased and somewhat excited to look at his.

And then his cousins started to show up.

"I don't have first cousins," he said. "At least, not that I know of." He laughed conspiratorially before he said, "But let's find out what either Aunt Harriet or Uncle Ricky could have been up to before the war."

"It seems to me they're discovering distant fifth-to-eighth cousins," Marchesa said. "What does that even mean? Actually, from a country like Scotland, wouldn't that imply you're related to almost everyone?"

"Oh. You ethicists. You're all so cynical. Look at Cynthia here," he said as he pointed to the DNA site on his computer screen. "Look at her photo. Just a head shot on the site, but doesn't she look like someone you'd like to have as a cousin?"

"Perhaps. But only if you wanted to pursue some kind of relationship with a possible, maybe, perhaps eighteen-year-old relative."

Andy sighed. "With these exciting results, aren't you even interested in sending in your sample? It's already paid for."

Later, Marchesa went to her desk to retrieve her test kit. She took it into their ensuite bathroom and read the instructions.

Do NOT eat, drink, smoke or chew gum for 30 minutes before

giving your saliva sample.

Easy enough, Marchesa thought. *I only do two of those things anyway.* She continued to read:

1. Fill the tube with saliva to the black wavy line.
Never thought I would have to spit at any time in my life.

2. Replace the funnel with the cap.
Funnel?

3. Tighten to release stabilizing fluid.
Stabilizing fluid?

4. Shake the tube for at least five seconds.
How long is five seconds?

5. Place the tube in the collection bag.
Get rid of this spit!

6. Mail in your sample.
Easy part.

Okay, I'll do it. Surprised it's not a cheek swab. Guess they needed to keep things simple.

~

When the message from FindYourOrigins appeared in her email several weeks later, Marchesa didn't really know what to do, how to respond. She'd almost forgotten she'd submitted the sample. Should she simply call Andy to be with her when she opened the message? *What am I nervous about? It's not like my DNA makeup is going to influence my life.*

She waited another week then finally decided to ask Andy to come from the sunroom of their condo to join her in her office. When they bought the condo, it was a four-bedroom unit, but without family of their own, they soon remodelled it to have a guest bedroom and two offices. Solarium was what Andy called it. *Solarium*, she thought. Reminded her of the various patient common rooms on each floor of the hospitals where she had worked.

When Andy joined her, he regarded her ethnicity estimate displayed on her screen. "Forty-five percent Italy, forty-five percent Greece, Turkey, Albania, Eastern Mediterranean."

"What does that actually mean? That I'm actually Greek or Turkish?"

"I suppose," Andy said, "there may not be enough data from that part of the world to come to definitive conclusions yet."

She realized Andy didn't know anything more about the DNA testing than she did. "But that's some of the oldest parts of the world when it comes to advancing civilizations."

"I agree, but advancing from where? There would be such a mixture of people from ancient times. As a geographer, I imagine FindYourOrigins simply hasn't yet tested sufficient samples from inhabitants of those regions to provide a broad database."

Marchesa frowned. "What do you mean?" she asked.

"Well, you know about the ongoing conflicts in the Balkans. Do you expect people to be interested in finding out what they think they already know and paying to do that? They're proud nations having survived the Ottoman empire, religious oppressions. Often forced to relinquish their pasts, their beliefs, their families. Now they are nation building, not DNA testing."

"Do you mean that stories handed down by parents, grandparents, community elders tell them all they need to know about where they came from?"

"Really, yes," Andy said. "Aside from that component, look at your ten percent 'Other.' You could actually be a Viking like me. After all, you mysteriously appeared in Scotland."

She instinctively skipped right past his musings and right on to her scientific analytics. "You know, Andy, I suddenly remember Drago saying di Mentone might not be an Italian name. Oh, that was such a long time ago."

"What did he say exactly?" Andy asked.

"You know, that was another lifetime. That was probably about sixty-five years ago."

"I don't suppose Drago would still be alive."

Marchesa looked bewildered. "When he was helping me, he had already lived about twenty years in Boston, arrived there as a teenager, then four or five years back in Italy. Then we wandered through Europe for almost two years."

"I guess if we add it up, he would have been in his forties when you last saw him. So," Andy paused as he did the mathematics, "if he were still alive, he'd be over one hundred. No, I don't think he is still alive."

31

ENGLAND 1947

"You will like them," Drago said. "They were friends of my family in Italy and friends with my uncle in Boston as well. Matteo is a baker just like my uncle."

"But Drago, I want to stay with you."

"We've talked about that, little one…"

"You haven't called me that for a long time."

"I'm sorry, Marchesa, but you know I've got permission to return to Boston next week. The embassy people were not able to give permission for you to travel with me."

"But…"

"I even said you were my niece. That we lost your papers."

"But I can stay here?"

"You are a refugee. Luckily, you have family already in Scotland. That's where they will be taking you."

"I know we talked about it, but how are they my family?"

"You must learn to be quiet, little one, not to ask so many questions. They are family because you are both Italian. Enough."

"How will I find you? When can I come to Boston?" Marchesa asked Drago.

32

SCOTLAND 1956

"I don't even know his surname," Marchesa told Andy. "Maybe, he was afraid I would become a liability, insist on immigrating to the U.S. Drago was with me to greet Matteo and Liliana at the King's Cross railway station. It surprised me that he didn't really seem to know them that well. I don't truly know how all this was arranged. Some kind of Italian magic, *chiaroreggenza* or intuition, I think."

"I certainly enjoyed our relationship with the Rosses," Andy said, looking back to that original meeting. "He admitted to me that their name was actually Rossi, but they changed it just before the war. Ross fit in Scotland. At least, it wouldn't draw unwanted attention during the war."

"They certainly treated me well. They were good parents."

"Too bad they didn't have children of their own."

Marchesa frowned and squinted her eyes. "We never talked about that. Although, they were open to talking about almost anything. They didn't seem to want to talk about Drago. I sensed they really didn't know each other. I came to recognize an Italian network within Britain."

"I'm surprised they didn't adopt you."

"We didn't know whether my family was alive or dead. They helped me search using the Red Cross. My father was definitely declared dead. My mother and sister presumed dead—not registered with the Red Cross or any of the other refugee records they accessed. I didn't continue to search."

33

TORONTO 2014

"Do you know anything about *FindYourOriginsDNA?*" Marchesa asked Chantal one morning at My Spot.

"Now there's a conversation starter," Chantal said. She and Richard had just arrived at the coffee shop, but Richard had left the table almost immediately and headed to the washroom.

"Sorry to be so abrupt. I wanted to ask you without Richard around. Not that I won't ask Richard too." Marchesa looked around the table to assess that she was still out of earshot of the few regulars who were at the restaurant so early. "Andy submitted his sample for testing and seemed to have fun with his results, but I never knew what his results meant. He didn't seem to have any close relatives. Only something like several hundred fifth-to-eighth cousins—what does that even mean?"

"I really don't know much about it. It's a swab you submit?"

"Actually, a sample of saliva. I presume everybody can come up with saliva. Maybe that's easier or more consistent than assuming individuals can take a proper swab."

Chantal laughed. "From what you're describing, it almost sounds like one of your ethical arguments you described to us."

"I didn't mean to do that. I'm sorry it sounded that way. I just don't know what my results mean."

Chantal nodded toward the corridor. "Richard's coming back now if you want to leave it just between us."

"I'm not sure. Let's leave it that way for now, okay? Thanks."

∽

A few days later, when all three of them were once again at My Spot, Chantal allowed the initial small talk to continue before she said, "Marsha, I hope you don't think I was betraying your confidence, but I told Richard you were asking what I knew about DNA testing. I explained that we weren't talking about any specific situations — just talking in general."

Before Marchesa could answer or look embarrassed or uncomfortable, Richard jumped in. "As it turns out," he said, "I've had some experience with DNA testing. I assume that's your interest and not some criminal prosecution testing."

Marchesa laughed and the tension left her face. She relaxed her pursed lips and started to smile. "Yes," she said, "ancestral not criminal. I was wondering about my husband's results with many fifth, sixth, or eighth cousins — wondering what all that could possibly mean."

"Well, you know my story — coming to Canada from Vietnam, American father who is unknown to me." Richard paused and smiled uneasily as he looked from Marchesa to Chantal and back again. "I sent my sample off by mail. Where's it go — Ireland, is it?"

Marchesa appreciated Richard's attempt to normalize what could otherwise have been a tense, embarrassing conversation. "That's right," she said. "Ireland."

No one said anything for a few moments, then Marchesa continued, "What I was saying about my confusion with my husband's…with Andy's results is…We joked that surely, with all those distant cousins, doesn't it simply mean he's related to all of Scotland?"

34

Marchesa regarded her computer screen, dumbfounded. She passingly covered her mouth with her left hand, then moved that hand to her throat. Very quickly, she shook her head, sat straight, and reached for her water glass, taking several sips to relieve her sudden dry throat.

She was looking at her DNA profile page for the first time in several weeks. *I haven't even explored this*, she thought. She was sure she'd become interested now following her recent conversations with Chantal and Richard. On other website visits, she had only seen her origin estimates, the percentages proscribed geographically. This day, however, there was something new.

The tabular breakdown was new to her. First cousin had an entry. Totally a surprise to Marchesa. Listed as A. A., 1st - 2nd Cousin, shared DNA: 330 cM across 17 segments.

Marchesa shook her head again, this time hoping to clear her mind. *What can this mean? I know what first cousin means, second, even third, but my family is all dead.*

She thought about what she knew of her parents' families. Not much, she decided, but surely anybody there would be reflected in her ten fourth-to-fifth cousins. *So few for me. Andy has five thousand plus on his record.*

She decided to print the few pages, thinking that she needed to be able to demonstrate what she needed to discuss. *Don't want to rely on my memory. This report is so simple, yet so complex.* Throughout her career, she had always liked to have all the indispensable paperwork immediately accessible when she needed to discuss or advise on a bioethics issue. It was always best to have everything close at hand.

I hope Richard and Chantal will be at the coffeeshop tomorrow. Or even just Richard. He seems to have a good idea of this stuff. I like it when they're there together. They make such a nice couple.

35

As she walked up Spadina and along Baldwin, she mentally rehearsed what she wanted to discuss. At one point, another pedestrian regarded her quizzically as she mumbled to herself. She sighed but realized that nowadays everyone seemed to be talking to themselves as they walked or ran, now that they had multiple Bluetooth schemes for their permanently connected mobile devices.

She was visibly disappointed when neither Chantal nor Richard were at the table. She checked her watch. *It's not because it's too early,* she thought. *That was a long game last night.* She had enjoyed the extra innings but realized the two of them had stories to file before they could call it a night. She had walked home quickly after the thirteenth inning, disappointed with the eventual Blue Jays loss. Bullpen pitching loaded the bases, and the Yankees were able to win with just a single in that final inning. A shame after Ricky Romero had pitched into the eight, and Bautista's home run had tied the game in the ninth. A shame, but exciting, nonetheless.

"Are you okay, Marsha?" Ben stood off her right shoulder and spoke quietly.

Marchesa realized she'd been scowling, so she tried to relax and rearrange her face into a smile. "I'm fine, thank you, Ben. Just mulling over last night's game. Thinking that because it was late, Richard isn't here yet."

"Oh, he won't be here this morning. He told me he'd be flying to Oakland for the weekend series."

"I thought he didn't like to travel to those away games."

"Usually, but a weekend in California can't be all that bad."

36

They really want to know more about Andy. They've started asking about my memories, Marchesa thought. *I thought baseball memories would satisfy them. I don't know what else to share. I think of him all the time. I'm not sure I want to share our personal or intimate moments yet. Maybe never. I regard them as friends now. Always, I'm pleased to see them. But they are reporters.*

It always amazed her that Andy relished taking in local sites when they travelled. But then he continued to describe himself as an economic geographer, so perhaps local colour fit that pattern.

Why she was suddenly reminiscing about this particular episode, she had no idea. It had only been a few years back when they spent a week in a seaside cottage in Maine. Well, hardly a cottage but a house Andy had rented from a colleague. Most of their travel had continued to be restricted to Canada where Andy loved looking for nuances, but as he said, the latitude of the place they planned to stay was actually north of most of what they knew as Southern Ontario. Definitely north of Toronto, maybe slightly south of Ottawa and Montreal. He maintained that Maine should actually be part of Canada. *He could really justify any of his knowing statements, couldn't he?* Marchesa thought.

∼

One morning, Andy had suggested they leave their cottage and drive to explore a nearby town. On the other days since they'd arrived, they spent relaxing and exploring the seacoast and the nearby hiking trails

"It's not that far from us," Andy said. "Maybe a half-hour drive. A nice little town—Wiscasset."

"And what would be our focus?" Marchesa knew Andy always had a focus, if not an ulterior motive.

"Wiscasset is in what they call the mid-coast region. The Sheepscot River flows through the town. We can walk around and look at some of the early American architecture."

He knew she loved scarves, and these craft boutiques were fun to browse.

"Then when we're ready for lunch, we can go to Red's Eats."

∼

And that's what we did, she thought now. *Spent the morning wandering around Wiscasset when our real intention was to visit the Red's Eats food truck.*

"I don't think calling it a food truck is fair," Andy said.

"What then?"

"It's called a take-out restaurant or a lobster shack based on what I've seen in tourist guides and local newspapers."

And we joined the line-up down the block and around the corner onto Water Street. In line for almost an hour and a half.

"This better be good," Marchesa said.

"They're reputed to serve the best lobster rolls in New England. All the best travel magazines say so."

"I don't even know what a lobster roll is."

"It's a bun filled with cooked lobster. In this case, the lobster is dressed with butter. Apparently, some places use mayo, but Red's serves over a pound of lobster drenched in butter."

Marchesa shuddered. "Are we even going to like this? I'm not that big on any seafood, as you know."

"Remember our lobster boat experience in New Brunswick?"

"Right you are. That was delicious. So fresh."

"And, when in Maine…"

Their turn came for ordering and pick-up.

"This is huge," Marchesa said. "I may not be able to eat it all."

"Any leftovers we'll take back to the cottage."

"I didn't realize it would be served cold. But it's delicious." She fumbled a bit to eat. It offended her that there were really no plates, just a polka dotted paper wrap. The lobster pieces sat randomly jutting out from the wrap. The pieces were bigger than her bite. She tried to dig in and opened her jaw as wide as possible to bite down. As a result, she became attached to lobster pieces by her teeth. Part hung out and her cheeks were bulging. Just then, Andy clicked, his phone in hand. She knew a good photographer would never embarrass a subject by taking a photo of them eating. When she detached herself from the beast, he showed it to her. He should have known she would be disgusted, and she was. More likely embarrassed. Andy smiled and told her he would delete it and forever forget what he saw as her beautiful face. He did just that.

"Maybe we can stop by on Friday for lunch when we're heading home," Marchesa said, and Andy nodded his agreement.

∽

This is the type of memory I think about. It brings me comfort, Marchesa thought. *As much as I enjoy being with Richard and Chantal, enjoy their company, talking with them, is this the sort of episode I want to relate to them when they ask questions about Andy?*

Or should I tell them things I remember so well like Andy taking me to Harrods when I saw that silk scarf. She had stopped dead in her tracks in the tile-lined aisle of the ladies' department. That beautifully gentle feel between her fingers when she stretched her hand forward and touched the scarf. She had an almost blinding flash of her mother on a spectacularly sunny day in Bergamo wearing what she remembered as that exact scarf, blowing gently from her neck. Andy bought the scarf for her even though it cost him more than an economist would pay for a week's groceries. A stunning Como silk scarf.

37

Marchesa looked at the arrangement of data on her screen. She grasped that she couldn't discuss or even question the presentation if she didn't make a better effort at understanding what was there. It was time to dismiss her alienation toward DNA testing and its results. She had actual personal results now even if she didn't understand what they meant.

Okay, first-to-second cousin? What does that even insinuate? My close family all died during the war. That's more than sixty... actually, close to seventy... years ago. How do I uncover what that means?

She looked again at her screen. Several entries as 4th - 6th Cousin. *That's distant. I know that, at least.* What was bothering her about her profile was the listing as 1st - 2nd Cousin with the initials A. A. *Those other distant cousins at least have full names. But A.A. shares significant DNA segments. That's meaningful. That's close. Hopefully Richard can help. Whenever he comes back.*

She had Richard's phone number, but she opted to discuss her printed profile information, to show him rather than try to describe it. *I don't know enough to talk about it over the phone.*

38

Marchesa was so pleased to see Richard already at the table when she arrived. Chantal wasn't there. She hoped they might have an opportunity to talk, just the two of them. She enjoyed Chantal's company and had come to consider her a friend, but sometimes...

"Good to see you, Richard. I hope your California trip was good. The games were a little late for me."

"Happy to see you too, Marsha. California was fine. I find it hard writing from there for those games. The time difference. But that's the reporting business."

Marchesa considered herself a student of facial expressions, but there was something she couldn't quite read in Richard's countenance — not a scowl but a twisting of his closed lips. And his eyes lit up almost in opposition to the rest of his facial appearance.

He's hiding something. What do they say? Something about spilling his guts. Ball's in his court. Marchesa chuckled at her deliberate use of idioms in her thoughts. She would never speak that way, but it gave her a certain amount of pleasure, as if it were her own private comedy routine.

"There was other business too. DNA business," he continued.

As she waited for him to expand, she realized she knew little of Richard's personal life. Except that he had been willing to discuss the immigrant experience with her, them both being from away.

From away, she thought. *Interesting that I've picked up that terminology. He really wants to talk. Maybe he's wishing Chantal were here, so he doesn't need to tell his story twice.*

"Just as well Chantal hasn't come today," he said, answering her unspoken question. "I'm not certain she's that interested in our DNA discussions."

"Did you find something out?"

"Sort of. I kinda lost my nerve though. About two months ago, I got a hit on my DNA page. The result came up as Parent/Child, and I don't know how well versed you are with the test site terminology." Richard looked at Marchesa, who gave a small shoulder shrug. "It said that 1800 centimorgans were shared. That's a very close relationship. And I guess the Parent/Child designation gives it away."

"What did you think?"

"Well, it provided two names, both with that designation. Brian Georgas and William Georgas. First, I checked the testing company site to see if they revealed where they lived in the world. Pinpointing location is at the user's discretion. I can show you what it looks like on the website world map. The initials BG indicated California as the location. I did an internet search of those names and realized, according to the results I had, that they both lived near Oakland. But, you know, that is so random that I worried if I had the right Georgas. So that's when I decided I would go to Oakland on business and file reports from that Blue Jays series against the Athletics."

"Then your father's name is Georgas, not Dixon?"

"Well, yes, but I didn't know that. My mother never shared that information with me."

"How common is the surname Georgas?"

"I don't know, but as far as I'm concerned, Bernie Dixon is my father. Just not biologically. My name is Dixon."

"Are your mother and...and father still alive?"

"Unfortunately, no. My mom died about seven years ago, and

Bernie didn't last long without her. They met shortly after we came to Canada. They were together about thirty years."

"I'm sorry to hear that." Marchesa touched Richard on the arm. She decided to save her own accounts for another time. *Good thing I left the papers in my purse*, she thought.

"I was hoping I'd discovered my American father, but I realized with these two guys—Brian and William—seeming to be about my age and with that sort of DNA relatedness, neither could be my father. These would be his children. My brothers…half-brothers, really."

"What did you do? This is exciting."

"Well…I had an address from the internet for Brian. I picked up a rental car. Drove there. Nice-looking modest house. So, no movie star. But then I didn't know what to do. Just go to the door like some sort of Vietnamese-Canadian stalker? What do I say? Hi, bro?"

"Wow! It is exciting!"

"There were three games in the series, so I drove by each day. Don't know what I was thinking. Just hoping maybe someone would be in the yard. So, maybe something more like a chance encounter."

"I don't know what to say," Marchesa said. "You must be disappointed."

"Yes and no. Now I think I've done the sensible thing. I went back to my DNA results page and clicked both *Contact Brian Georgas* and *Contact William Georgas* to use the message feature. There's no reply yet, but I'll wait. It's the more sensible thing to do. Don't know if you know me well enough yet, but it's not really my style to go off half-cocked."

That's what I will do as well, she thought. *Just click the* Contact A.A. *link and see what happens.*

39

"Richard, I don't know what to do next." Marchesa looked across the table to where Richard was talking with Chantal.

"You sound desperate, Marsha. Are you okay?"

"Sorry to interrupt your conversation, but I heard you say you needed to leave. I am maybe not desperate, but certainly frustrated. My apologies, Chantal." She nodded at Chantal as she spoke.

"What can I ... or maybe I should say we ..." He tilted his head toward Chantal who nodded with agreement. "How can we help?"

Marchesa pushed a single printed page across to the two of them. "You see here that via the DNA testing site, I have had contact from my supposed cousin."

Chantal read from the paper.

I am interested to establish how we may be related.

She showed Richard. "Funny, they don't give a name or how to contact them."

"Oh, I've had experience with this," Richard said. "You simply continue to contact through the testing site. You know, the same way as they contacted you."

"Why?"

"It protects them until they are assured you are legitimate and interested in exploring further," explained Richard.

"Legitimate? It's through DNA profiles. I don't know what is more legitimate than DNA."

"Yes, but understand, Marsha, because your field was bioethics, you appreciate contested arguments. Because of your healthcare and science background, you know that DNA profile results are hardly contestable."

"Also," Chantal said, "just because DNA testing has taken off in demand, people being tested may not know what to expect. Their only context may be TV crime shows."

"Yes," Marchesa said, "I suppose as with ethics, when something like test results are challenged, I don't often ask but always wonder, why did you order the test if you are not going to believe the results.?"

"And it's like my situation with the California Georgas boys," Richard said. "I have a reply with kind of a *how can we believe your story* attitude. You're Vietnamese—how can your DNA be the same as ours?"

"Again, why did they, both brothers, send their DNA samples in?" Marchesa asked.

"It's all the rage, especially with some age groups," Richard said. "Why did I get mine done? Why did you get yours done?"

"It certainly begs the question."

Chantal looked from Richard to Marchesa and back again. "So, Richard, ball's in your court. Why did you submit your test kit?"

"It's simple, really. I know I have an American father. I wondered whether he might have submitted a test as well. I wondered whether he even knew my mother was pregnant, though she assures me she didn't tell him. She says he was posted back home before she showed any signs."

"And you, Marsha?" Chantal looked toward Marchesa.

40

Marchesa was looking forward to further DNA discussion. However, she was the first to arrive at their table that morning. The restaurant was nearly empty. She glanced toward the wall clock and realized how early she was.

She looked toward the door, shook her head, took a second glance, and there was Leanne. Leanne had come up in a conversation with Ben a week or so previously. Marchesa assumed she had gone back to Boston, but Ben knew she had been very busy at work since the storm.

"Leanne works at one of the downtown hospitals," Ben had said. "She works part time in the pharmacy."

"Which hospital, do you know?"

"No, I don't know, but I suspect Mount Sinai because of some of the talk I heard. And, of course, how close we are here on Baldwin Street. But, you know, now she comes in after her work rather than in the morning. And, of course, nobody from the morning big table is here, so she sits near the window just the way she used to."

And then, there she was.

Leanne came right to the chair beside Marchesa. Marchesa flinched a bit, alarmed by Leanne's abrupt and brazen approach. Leanne sat and blurted out, without any other acknowledgement, "You have essential tremor."

"Pardon...wha...what?"

"Essential tremor. You hide your hand, but I can see it in your neck."

Marchesa put her right hand to that side of her neck and felt what she was coming to recognize as a gentle shake, more pronounced now that she was being called out.

"Are you on medication for it?"

Marchesa shook her head. "No." She continued to be puzzled by this bizarre interaction.

"The reason I ask," Leanne said, "is one of our hospitals is developing a new procedure to eliminate the tremor when conventional pharmaceuticals have failed."

"What sort of procedure?"

"It's called focussed ultrasound. Just being developed now at Sunnybrook. Soon they'll be enrolling patients in the study. But first you need to try conventional treatments."

"How do you know this? What's your interest?"

"I work parttime in several hospital pharmacies to fill in when they are short staffed."

"You're a pharmacist?"

"I work as a pharmacy assistant. My credentials from Massachusetts are not accepted here without writing the provincial licensing exams."

"Would that require going back to school?"

"A short orientation course, but I don't want to work fulltime anyway."

Leanne then got up from her chair and moved toward the door, but not before putting her index finger to her temple and saying what Marchesa interpreted as "Zap."

∼

Wasn't that just the strangest encounter, thought Marchesa. *Leanne said more, used more words than the total exchanged in all those months I've known her. Why the sudden interest? Oh, good, here come Richard and Chantal. Time for DNA talk ... no more tremor talk.*

41

"Well, good morning, Marsha. I bet you're surprised to see me again so soon. Not my usual pattern, eh? Coming here every day."

"I am glad to see you, Richard. We had such an interesting talk about DNA yesterday."

"By the way, we just bumped into Leanne on the street. Looked like she had just left here. I tried greeting her, but she was just as uncommunicative as usual." Richard shrugged his shoulders and looked toward Chantal.

Chantal had been smiling toward Marchesa during the whole preliminary exchange. "Richard and I may be working together on a story we're excited about," she said, changing the topic at hand.

Richard took over. "And we'd like to use your expertise in ethics if you're willing."

Marchesa said nothing for a moment. *There goes our DNA talk*, she thought. "You realize I'm retired. Possibly very outdated on current thought."

"Oh," Richard said. "This may be mainly memory of past events. Maybe some speculation too. Why don't I start from the beginning..."

Chantal sang barely under her breath, *Let's start from the very beginning...*

Richard fashioned a mock stern look on his face and glared at her but had trouble holding back a laugh. "See what I have to put up with," he said to Marchesa. "Don't know why I even talk to this woman."

Wow, Marchesa thought. *If they're not partners yet, they will be soon.*

Richard continued, "It's actually a very serious topic. I ran into someone unexpectedly in the press box about a week ago. Marv Edwards, his name. A friend from way back when we were both investigative reporters. He still is but doesn't write sports. And from what I remember, not the least bit interested in sports. Yet there he was, at a Blue Jays game. I soon realized he was there to see me."

Wow, he's so wound up. He's never talked this much around me. Marchesa hadn't realized until then that the table was empty except for them. To her relief, others weren't there to overhear their banter.

"Once he explained what he was looking for, I introduced him to Chantal. Now the three of us are planning to, at least, work together to map out a possible story about the impact on sports, baseball in particular, as the model for handling a possible … mmm … possible disaster or, how did he term it?"

"Possible catastrophic events," Chantal said. "Marv was interested in what was discussed in Olympic team tryouts. I was still a hopeful for the Canadian ski team leading up to the Sarajevo Olympics. Even at that stage, before selections were made, there were lectures on what could possibly happen because of the hostilities in Yugoslavia. What would we do if something untoward happened, and I remember wondering about the use of the word *untoward*. But it became legitimized later when I worked in post-war Kosovo."

"Were they concerned about something like the massacre during the Munich Olympics?" Marchesa asked Chantal.

"That, and because this was the Winter Olympics, the possibility of a flu epidemic or something like that."

"Now, that's the sort of thing I was wondering about," Richard said. "Infectious disease outbreaks and what is done to prepare contingency plans. That and events like 9/11. We weren't sure how to approach you or whether it would even be appropriate. That's why I didn't say anything last night."

"What sort of questions do you have, Richard?"

"Well, let's start with 9/11. September 11th was a Tuesday. Major League Baseball usually has a full schedule Tuesdays. And this was no exception. The trade centre attacks were that morning. The MLB commissioner very quickly cancelled the Tuesday games, and then, by the end of the day, cancelled all games for the rest of the week. They were to resume the following Monday. To my mind, it was a very appropriate response. Now, my question is, was this part of an MLB contingency or a spur of the moment, seat of the pants decision by the commissioner?"

"You know," said Marchesa, "at the time, amongst my colleagues, we discussed that suspending a baseball game was trivial and almost immoral. That opinion changed quite quickly, though, when we recognized an attempt to return to some semblance of order. Also, I don't know whether you know, but I remember that many of the Yankee players walked around downtown and near the Trade Centre talking to people, comforting them. Showing their own shock."

"Do you think they were encountering rage?" Chantal asked.

"Not immediately. The immediate concern seemed to be for safety and community. That's what brought my colleagues back on board in their analysis and responses."

"So, resumption of play was seen as the proper course?"

"Essentially, yes! A diversion, a contemplation of normality. Although, as bioethicists, we don't like the term *normality*."

"I guess I'm thinking about planning," Richard said. "In your work, did you plan for catastrophic events? I mean, I'm trying to remember. Was it 2009 when we expected a very major avian flu outbreak? Did you plan for the possibilities and eventualities?"

Marchesa thought for a moment or two. "I was retired by then, but I was called back as a resource person for the Ottawa hospitals group. Mind you, ethicists are not the movers-and-shakers who develop logistical plans. We comment on whether planned moves are appropriate just as the legal department would comment on whether the plans are legal."

"What other planning did you do for events in the past?"

"The one that immediately comes to mind is the early eighties, the worry about AIDS and whether that was some kind of end-of-the-world scenario. That's my first memory of permanent committees being formed. They began calling them pandemic preparedness committees."

"And they still exist?"

"Absolutely!"

"One reason I thought of asking you about hospital response was that I broke my glasses," Richard said. He paused, taking in the puzzled look on Marchesa's face, then laughed and said, "That may not make sense to you. I broke the frame of my so-called frameless glasses. I tried to glue them back together but that didn't work. According to my optician, there is no easy fix. New frame is the only cure."

Boy is he ever loquacious. Marchesa glanced at Chantal, but from her expression, she realized Chantal had already heard the story.

"So, that's the background. I made an appointment for an eye exam because I was sure I needed a new prescription. In the meantime, I have several old pairs of glasses in my night table. The pair I selected has a yellow sticky note on the case saying *SARS passed*. So, even though our story will concern MLB preparations for catastrophic events, I wondered what public institutions would do to prepare. Not so much how they respond, but what they do in preparation."

"My experience with SARS, AIDS before that, then avian flu was really with the what-if planning," Marchesa said. "As I recall... Andy was the baseball fan of the family at the time of SARS. And SARS was a Toronto-centred outbreak. Major League Baseball talked of teams not playing in Toronto, but perhaps the Blue Jays playing in the opponents' home parks. Nothing much really happened because the World Health Organization downgraded warnings within the first couple of weeks of the baseball season."

"That's how I recall it too," Richard said. "Chantal?"

"I was in Kosovo at the time covering the former Yugoslavia for *The Star*. And maybe dealing with *real* life-and-death matters."

"Now, now, Chantal."

"So, where did you get the label for your glasses case, Richard?"

"Sorry, Marsha, I should have completed that story. March 2003, my former wife had knee surgery for an old injury."

Former wife, he said. Hmmm... interesting.

"When I visited her in the hospital, I wasn't allowed through the door until I had answered a questionnaire about travel and possible current symptoms suggestive of SARS," Richard explained.

"And you kept the sticker?"

"Just a souvenir."

"Of your marriage?" Marchesa asked.

"No, no. Epidemics always interested me. I was pretty young at the time, but I remember some of the neighbours scaring me with their stories of growing up during polio."

42

"I'm sorry, Marsha, that we didn't get to your DNA questions the other day. I had to get on my way so I could fly to Kansas City for the series with the Royals."

"That's okay, but I do hope you can help me with what I have."

"We'll certainly get to that," Richard said. "But first..."

Oh, oh, but first.

"I'd like to tell you what I found out about Blue Jays contingency planning. It turns out they do have plans for tragedies like terrorists or infectious pandemics. And pandemics is their planning word, not mine."

"That's reassuring."

Richard paused while Ben placed their coffees in front of them. "Of course, I've discussed this with Chantal." Richard nodded to Chantal, then looked at the others at their table, and around the restaurant. "It's probably not a total secret, but I need to treat it as confidential while we're researching and writing."

Marchesa nodded her agreement. She tried not to show the disappointment she was feeling in her facial expression.

"I'm glad they have plans, or at least have discussed plans. I haven't found out yet whether they are on board with MLB or whether this is only a Blue Jays planning process." Richard stretched his shoulders and reached for his coffee mug. Marchesa took advantage of his pause to sip hers as well.

"Anyway, the only thing I wanted to say is they seem willing to play games with an empty stadium if that seems necessary and appropriate."

"Not simply cancel the games like the week after September 11th?" asked Marchesa.

"They're worried about contractual obligations—not just player salaries but television revenues and staff salaries. Here's something I've been visualizing, but don't laugh until I've explained my concept, okay?"

"Sure, okay with me."

Richard looked at Chantal's face until she nodded her agreement as well.

"I don't know the effect on players of playing in an empty stadium," Richard continued. "Of course, they could turn the sound system on with some sort of contrived sound of fans cheering, but the stadium is still empty. What if they fill the stadium with life-size cut-outs of individual fans?"

"What?" Marchesa asked.

"Of course, the fans would have to pay to display their likenesses."

"I would never do that!" Marchesa shrugged her shoulders and looked toward Chantal.

"What if that fee went to charity? After all, you have a distinctive television image," Richard asked.

"You mean like the Jays Care Foundation?"

"Yes."

"Well, maybe if it was for charity, Richard." Marchesa agreed.

43

Marchesa was hoping against hope that today she could discuss her anxieties and, quite frankly, her lack of knowledge and uneasiness about how to go forward, or even continue being bothered, with her DNA profile.

She arrived first but soon after she took her place at the table and greeted the others already seated, she saw Richard through the window. Standing out front, perhaps enjoying the morning sunshine that was enveloping him in a shaft of brilliance. Marchesa surmised he was anticipating Chantal's arrival.

Before long, they came in, both smiling as they acknowledged Marchesa and the others. Marchesa considered Richard to assess his mood. *He's quieter today*, she thought. *Back to his customary self. Perhaps DNA talk today.*

Marchesa decided to follow her habitual approach and lingered until Ben delivered their coffees. Her uneasiness almost got the better of her. She waited for the usual repartee between Richard and Ben before speaking.

"I brought copies of my paperwork," she said. She chastised herself almost before she finished speaking. *Paperwork! Why didn't I just say what I meant? Why do I do that? It's my DNA results, I meant.*

She drew several folded sheets of paper from her handbag and placed them on the table. She unfolded them and ran her hands over the length of the pages to flatten them. "There," she said. "You may be wondering why there's suddenly a hurry, but this is bothering me."

Richard nodded his head and smiled, then looked at Chantal as if seeking her approval as well. Chantal nodded her head.

Chantal is game for anything, thought Marchesa. *Richard is the one I need in agreement.*

"Let's look at these," said Richard. He reached across and pulled the several pages toward him.

Marsha, you have a DNA match to explore.

FindYourOrigins.com

To: marshamacgregor@hotmail.com

You have an unviewed DNA match.
A.A. (1990 —)
1st — 2nd cousin

"Wow, Marsha," Richard said and pushed Marchesa's papers toward Chantal. He continued, "You told me before that you were confused about the meaning of your results. You realize matches of this sort could be cousins, aunts, uncles, as well great-aunts and great-uncles, great-nieces and great-nephews."

"Really, that broad?"

"Yes, but still an indicator of a closely related person in terms of DNA sequencing," Richard said. "Now the question comes, what have you done with this?"

"Nothing really except stew about it. What does it mean?"

"Maybe we should find a different place to discuss this." Chantal subtly moved her head to indicate their tablemates, none of whom were yet showing any particular interest in their discussion.

Marchesa creased her brow and frowned. "I just want to talk about this, " she said. "It's really playing on my mind to the point of disturbing my sleep."

"We'll find a good place to talk," Richard said. He stood up and approached the counter. He stretched to look behind the small display case on the counter and signalled to Ben in the food prep area.

Ben appeared surprised and pulled out his order pad in a move to prepare their bills.

"Is there some place the three of us could go to talk privately? Like your office?"

"You mean you want to go down to the basement?"

"Is it okay to use your office?"

"You can use it, but is Marsha okay on the stairs?"

"Chantal and I can help her, if necessary."

Their friends prepared to wish them a good day as the three of them stood and moved from their seats. Some looked perplexed as the trio moved toward the basement door. One or two mouths hung open, others raised their eyebrows in surprise. The basement was an area none had been to or experienced.

Marchesa had been apprehensive about climbing down basement or, as she thought about them, cellar steps. She was pleased to note that the run of each step was adequate for her, about nine inches, comfortable for her small feet. The rise she noted was not too steep, and there was a solid banister. She could do this without the help of Richard and Chantal, though each expressed willingness to assist.

Run and rise, she thought. *Didn't Andy impress upon me to always use the proper terms? But* banister, *isn't that just a little formal for this piece of metal pipe? It's just a handrail.*

Richard directed them toward a small room that had been set up as an office. The rest of the basement was a storage area with modern-looking shelving. Marchesa didn't take the time to look around other than to register a positive first impression of organization and cleanliness. Richard directed them into the office. He offered her the seat behind the desk, but she demurred. As well as the desk, the small room was set up with two filing cabinets and three other chairs.

"Why don't we just sit here?" Richard suggested, continuing to take his lead role.

Let's just get to this discussion. It's driving me crazy, Marchesa thought as she sat in one of the chairs.

Richard reached across the table and pulled Marchesa's printed pages toward him. "Let's see what we have here," he said. "You did say your potential match used only initials. Have you contacted him...or her?"

"No, I wanted to wait until we had the time to examine this. I knew you had experience with your discovery of half-brothers. And I trust your judgement."

Chantal leaned over to look at the printouts. "Your e-mail is Marsha MacGregor."

"Yes."

"That's your married name. From what you've told us, you don't know if any of your relatives survived. So, your married name would not be recognizable by a geographically distant relative...I may be jumping to conclusions here...an Italian relative."

Marchesa sat still with a look of shock, or maybe realization, on her face. "I see," she said. "I understand what you're saying."

"I'm only concerned that this contact may not expect or may not believe a message that appears to be from someone of Scottish descent who is claiming to be a relative. I mean, first or second cousin is very close."

"At the same time," Richard said. "This person isn't using initials because they don't know who Marsha is. They're using A.A. in the profile to protect their own privacy, I would guess."

"So, where do I go from here? What are my next steps?"

Chantal and Richard spoke at the same time with practically the same words, advising her to use her account on the FindYourOrigins website to contact A.A. They explained how contacting someone on the website protects her identity, as there is no sharing of email addresses.

"What do I say?"

Richard started to make notes on one of Marchesa's pages. "Provide your real name, sorry…I mean your birth name."

"Okay, Marchesa di Mentone…"

It was Chantal's moment to look surprised. "You mean like the Edgar Allan Poe character?"

"Apparently so."

"Sorry to jump in like that…I knew Marchesa was your name, but I'd never heard your surname."

"Then," Richard said, "getting back to the issue at hand. I'm Marchesa from whatever city you came from. Like, I'm Marchesa from Milan."

"Okay, introduce myself as someone from Bergamo. Maybe then my parents' names."

"I think that's exactly how to approach it. Chantal, what do you think?"

"I think you're right, Richard, the way Marchesa described it."

Richard turned toward Marchesa. "What name would you prefer us to use?"

"I'm so used to being Marsha now. I really don't know what to say. The group at My Spot seems like they'd be comfortable either way."

"Can't really describe them as a cosmopolitan group," Richard said. "But a name's a name. They'd be happy with whichever you prefer."

"I think we're becoming sidetracked again," Chantal said quietly.

"Thank you both," Marchesa said. "I think I know how to proceed. Then I guess we wait and see what the response is."

44

My name in FindYourOrigins, as you see, is Marsha MacGregor. My birth name is Marchesa di Mentone, originally from Bergamo, Italy. My parents were Tommaso di Mentone (born April 10, 1905, died 1945) and Abigaille Giovanni (born September 16, 1911, died ?).

Weeks passed. She realized she might not receive a reply from someone who was using only initials to make contact. Then, miraculously, it happened: she received a response from A.A.

Are you related to Albertina di Mentone?

My sister? Is this a joke? This must be a scam. But where did they dredge up her name? Dead since the war — how heartless!

45

"What do I do...I mean, how do I deal with this?" Marchesa looked directly at Richard, then turned to Chantal for help. "Albertina was my sister. She died with my mother during the war as we were escaping from Italy. This must be a scam!"

"You're sure she died?"

"We searched through all the available agencies and archives of displaced persons to find my mother and sister for several years."

"We?"

"Drago and I." Marchesa paused. "I'm sure I told you about Drago. Once he left me with the Rosses, they helped me do more searches through the National Archives in Edinburgh. There were not many Italian records available."

"What is your main concern?" Richard asked.

"I'm not certain. My family is dead. That's what I believe to be true. Yet now a question of close relatives comes up."

"I'm no expert on DNA testing results, but my own experience tells me interesting facts and developments can be unearthed. I mean, who would have imagined I have American family?"

"Do I just answer? What if it is some scam?"

Chantal smiled. "I understand your concern, but perhaps this is a relative trying to build a family tree or something like that."

"I don't really know why I'm afraid to take the next step."

"There's no necessity, you know," Richard said. "But it's like you said when we talked about ethics, a legitimate question is, why did you have this testing done if you don't want to consider the results? I know you were talking about medical tests, but I think the same principles apply. Listen to me propound...Principles, indeed!"

"Don't you want to know what your relationship is?" asked Chantal.

"I know what you and Richard mean, Chantal. I don't know what to do. I don't know if I want to do anything. I don't understand why I feel that way."

"Do you know what you fear?" Chantal reached for Marchesa's hand. "You're shaking. This really has you upset."

"I was incredibly excited when I received my results and could hardly contain myself." She looked at Richard. "But then I realized I only have initials so far."

"Then, maybe you should take the initiative and ask for a name," said Richard. "After all, DNA doesn't lie. You have a very close relative."

∼

Then, Marchesa received the most extraordinary message:

My name is Alessandros Audisio. My parents are Marco Audisio and Donna Accardo. My grandparents are Herberto Grimaldi and Albertina di Mentone.

Marchesa was aghast—Albertina? *My sister is dead!*

She put everything down and sat in front of her computer, dumbfounded.

I wish Andy were here. He wouldn't believe it either, but at least I could tell him I'm scared.

A long time passed, and she finally returned from a place where time had stopped. She had no idea how long that had been. She gathered herself from the initial shock and forced herself to read on.

You mentioned being in Canada in one of your messages.

Where in Canada are you?

∽

She could hardly qualify her disbelief, but it felt real once she shared everything with Richard and Chantal.

"He's writing in good English," Marchesa said to Richard. "He must be in the U.S. or Canada."

"Or the U.K.... or Europe," Richard suggested.

"What do you think I should do?"

"Have you looked at his name?"

"What do you mean?"

"Alessandros Audisio..." Richard stopped himself because suddenly, when he explained that he had had that overwhelming feeling of unbelievable coincidence that makes the hairs on your neck stand up, Chantal said, "You mean Audisio, the Red Sox first baseman?"

"Such a stretch. That's like saying Ricky Romero and Juan Carlos Romero are brothers just because of their names," Richard replied to Chantal's question.

Marchesa was shocked but gathered herself and became determined to follow through.

∽

She decided to take the plunge and open a dialogue.

I live in Toronto.

The reply came quickly.

I travel to Toronto several times a season. Could we meet?

I must be very closely related.

Several times a season? That's an unusual way to talk about travel. Must be an old person.

Yes, we can meet.

Marchesa's hand shook uncomfortably. She felt she might collapse. She pondered for the whole day where they could meet that would be neutral territory. Not her condo—she didn't want him to know where in Toronto she lived. Maybe on a bench by the waterfront—but that would be so weather dependent. *I know*, she thought, *a coffee at My Spot. That name seems so ironic. No, too many of the regulars and Ben and Sally to see me with a strange man. Maybe he would like to come to a Jays game. Next home game is Tuesday.*

So, she set it up. He agreed to meet her at the game. He was familiar with the Rogers Centre. She described her seat location and the private concourse to her seats where they could meet.

Wow! Those are pretty exclusive seats. How did you score those? Usually only royalty get that privilege. Could a relative of mine be royalty?

Tuesday came and she could hardly function in anticipation of their meeting. It was a quarter to six in the evening when she arrived uncharacteristically early. She could hear the crack of the bats as batting practice was wrapping up. People were coming through the gates and wandering through the concourse, buying memorabilia, popcorn, beer. Hard to imagine they needed more memorabilia since nearly everyone was dressed in blue with Dickey, Encarnacion, Rasmus emblazoned on the back of their jerseys. Jays hats of all sorts were worn on their heads—blue with white, blue with dark blue, double blue, light blue like the home jerseys, favourite player names and numbers here and there.

She positioned herself close to her seats with an eye to the narrow concourse. She saw a shadow, then a man. It was a player, a player in a Boston uniform coming toward her. He was smiling.

When he got close, he said, "Hi, I'm Alessandros Audisio."

Of course, she recognized him. She always made sure to be at the game when the Jays played the Red Sox, one of her favourite opposing teams.

"I bet you're surprised!"

Marchesa felt she might collapse. He steadied her with his hands on her shoulders and apologized for presuming surprise might be a good opening. He tried to lighten the mood by offering to sign an autograph for her. Other fans worked their way around Alessandros and her to get to their seats in the same area. He quietly touched her arm.

"I have a game to play. Can I see you after? I want so much to know you." In a hushed voice he leaned into her and said, "Who knew I could have a great-aunt right here behind home plate?"

What a monumental shock. Marchesa's hand shook uncontrollably.

∼

Richard and Chantal were also blown away as Marchesa reported her results to them. They were both surprised that Richard's jump to Sandros being the identified first or second cousin was more than a premonition. They were so eager to meet him with Marchesa. Over the next two days, Richard and Marchesa arranged to meet Sandros on-field in front of the visiting team dugout before the final Blue Jays–Red Sox game of the series. Richard agreed to arrange entrance to the park before the gates opened using his press privileges. He explained that they would enter through Gate 9, though instead of turning toward the press box, they would walk straight to the field.

"They know me there," he said. "I often set up interviews there before a game."

And just as he predicted, they passed through quickly. Richard and Chantal were greeted by name, but so was Marchesa.

"Good afternoon, Mrs. MacGregor," the usher said. "You're here early today." Marchesa simply smiled in greeting.

Richard later asked how they knew her name.

"Ah," Marchesa said. "They know."

Richard asked, "Do they know you sit behind home plate?"

46

Marchesa had asked Sandros whether she could bring two friends to meet him. When she admitted they were both sports journalists, he seemed a little leery. Once she explained that he had been interviewed by Richard Dixon, he seemed relieved and enthusiastically agreed.

Sandros hurried toward her, and with a quiet, warm intonation said, "Aunt Marchesa."

"Oh, Alessandros," she replied. "How wonderful to see you again." Then she felt that weakness in her legs as the built-up adrenaline drained from her after the nervousness of their initial meeting.

Sandros looked uncertain after that awkward moment as well. He approached her, arms open wide in the gesture of someone very familiar looking for a hug.

Marchesa introduced Sandros to Richard and Chantal. Sandros smiled in recognition of Richard and graciously shook Chantal's outstretched hand.

When Marchesa introduced him as Alessandros, he interrupted and said, "Actually, most of my teammates just call me Sandros. I kinda like it. When I was in China, I wasn't very good with the language and was never sure of the names I was called. Whether they were even polite. At least here I speak the language. And the Red Sox are great teammates."

"We have so much to talk about," Marchesa said. She thought they should allow the conversation to develop naturally, but she was really anxious and preoccupied to know about Albertina.

~

"Your English is so good. Where did you grow up?"

"In Rome and in Washington. My father was a diplomat. For a long time, he was Italy's Ambassador to the United States. I went to a school in Maryland for children of diplomats."

Though Marchesa had become practiced in comportment, she almost blurted out, "You say Albertina is your grandmother. My sister is still alive?"

"Yes, yes, most assuredly so! She is my *Nonna*."

Sandros reached over to steady Marchesa by touching her arm.

"*Nonna* lives in Bergamo," he continued once Marchesa seemed to have recovered emotionally. "She has never seen me play baseball. I played in China and Japan for several years. It did not seem feasible for her to travel there to see me play. I really didn't have proper accommodation for her to visit me. Things are different here. She feels safe to come to Boston or Toronto. When I tell her I've met you, she will be blown away and probably be on the next plane."

"She lives in Bergamo?"

"Not the old family house. It was destroyed. It's a newer house on the same street. Well, I guess not such a new house now. It was built after the war, long before I was born. I think long before my mother was born too."

"How is she?" Her disbelief transported her to Bergamo, to her childhood, to the war, to the camp, to her last vision of Albertina.

"Her husband was Mayor of Bergamo for a long time."

"When would that have been?"

"Nineteen-seventies, I think. Again, long before I was born. I just know because it was a point of pride in family discussions when family got together."

Marchesa stepped back from the others. She was glad Richard

and Chantal had stayed to join her after the game and hoped either one of them would take over the banter. *What a lot to absorb*, she thought. She looked around the stadium, comparing the view from the field to what she was able to see from her own seats. Then she became engrossed with the playing surface of artificial grass. She bent over to extend her hand and feel the surface. When she stood again, she felt dizzy and was temporarily breathless.

Chantal moved toward her, gently took her arm, and quietly said, "Do you want to sit down? We can go over there." Chantal pointed toward the dugout.

"I'm fine. I shouldn't bend over like that." Marchesa looked at Sandros and Richard, who were deep in conversation. *They don't even realize I was having trouble.* She smiled at Chantal, who seemed to be able to read her mind. She overheard Richard calling him Sandros.

Sandros. I like Sandros as a name. Suits him. But I want to know much more about Albertina.

47

"*Affrettatevi figlia! Adesso!*" Tommaso had yelled. "It is raining. This is good. It will hide us. Hurry Marchesa. *Mamma e Albertina sono andati prima.*"

Marchesa remembered trying to make her way over the slick mud surface of the compound, stepping with extreme care to maintain her balance and avoid slipping. She fought to keep her eyes at least partially open in the driving rain. She remembered the lightning illuminating the line of people trying to escape the prison camp through a newly created gap in the fence.

She remembered all this while walking toward the baseball stadium. She was both elated and in disbelief that she'd now be able to watch Sandros play. A member of her own family. A family she didn't know existed.

So much has happened, changed since Sandros appeared. I'm so happy Andy pressed me to try DNA testing. But now while he's in Toronto, Sandros wants us to phone my sister…Albertina. I don't even know her. I looked after her in the camp. Mama wasn't able—depressed. But that was so long ago. She was seven years old the last time I saw her. I hurried to catch up with them outside the fence. Drago looked for them but said he couldn't find them. He was so good to me. I wonder if he thought a depressed woman and a seven-year-old child would be too much trouble, maybe impede our escape—mine and his.

Stop that. Don't start doubting Drago now. He kept me safe. I migrated into this safe, happy life through his efforts. Almost seventy years ago now. I wish we'd been able to keep in touch. It was strange when the Rosses, his so-called family friends, didn't know how to reach him.

And Andy offered to take me to Boston to see if we could search for him. What stopped me? Maybe worry that my life had become so good and maybe Drago's hadn't.

Marchesa realized she had better pay attention rather than be lost in her reminiscences as she approached the ballpark. She needed to get to her seat. Again she was deliberately early. She always enjoyed watching the players warm up. She enjoyed the camaraderie on display, the competitive spirit even for stretching and limbering up. Also, she wanted to ensure Sandros would see that she was there.

When Sandros finished a set of stretches, he waved at her and jogged over to the wall just below her seat.

"Aunt Marchesa," he said. "*Buongiorno*." He pointed to the open roof and the blue sky. "What a great day for baseball."

"Good luck, Sandros."

"Don't you worry. We'll take care of these Blue Jays."

Several of her section booed good-naturedly, then laughed and high-fived each other. One yelled, "Go Jays Go!" They collectively regarded Marchesa with a *Wow! You know this guy!*

"Are you still good for the phone call when the game's over?"

"Yes! Absolutely, for certain! We'll go to my place!" She smiled shyly, looking around proudly at the others who'd observed her interaction with Sandros. "My nephew," she said. "Grand-nephew, I mean."

48

"So, how did the phone call go?" Richard asked. "It was so good of Sandros to arrange for you to call your sister."

"Oh, I'm almost speechless," Marchesa smiled at the two of them. "That Sandros is so kind." She laughed. "I never thought of it before the phone call, in the lead-up to talking with Albertina. She speaks very little English. There I am, I've lived virtually exclusively in English for almost seventy years. I've spoken French when we were in Montreal and Ottawa. Almost no Italian."

"Was it hard to communicate?" Chantal asked.

"Well, you know, Chantal, she spoke so fast. Luckily, Sandros translated for both of us. Strange, not speaking the same language as my own sister."

They sat quietly for a few minutes while Ben refreshed their coffees. Ben paused to allow her to reconsider when she'd ordered her first unadorned coffee. She wasn't going to change that order now.

"Did you speak Italian when you were with your stepparents in Scotland?"

"No, Richard, they were so concerned about everyone thinking they were Scottish. Especially that soon post-war. Afterall, they had changed their name from Rossi to Ross even before the war. So no, we spoke no Italian."

"So, you haven't spoken Italian for the time you've been living in English." Richard laughed. "Which is somewhat longer than I've been living in English."

Marchesa was perplexed by Richard's statement until Chantal

angled her head at her and joined Richard's laughter. *Of course, of course, he's younger than I am. That's funny.*

"I assume you're going to get together again. For another call, I mean," Chantal said.

"Yes, indeed. But actually, Sandros is hoping to fly her to Toronto rather than Boston for one of the times he plays here."

"Wow," Richard said. "That would be great."

"I have a spare bedroom in my condo so she can stay with me. Of course, she'll be here to visit her grandson as well as me. But Sandros lives in a hotel when he's in town."

"When do you think this will happen?" Chantal asked.

"Could be awhile. She doesn't have a passport. From what I gleaned today, her husband died probably around the same time as Andy. I might not have a passport either if our new ones hadn't had a ten-year expiry date. I still don't want to travel alone, not without Andy."

48

"You know," Richard said, "Except for baseball, I don't think we've talked very much about Andy."

"Andy was my guardian angel. Perhaps my second guardian angel, but my lifetime one."

"You mentioned the man who guided you through Europe as a guardian angel…" Chantal said.

"Drago."

"Ah, yes, that's it. Does that mean you believe in angels because you refer to them as such?" Chantal asked.

Marchesa laughed. "Certainly not in a religious sense. My early experiences of how good Catholics destroyed my family killed religion for me. I couldn't imagine being a believer after that. Mind you, I went to church with the Rosses in Edinburgh. Catholic, of course. That was how they had been raised. But they were not true believers. It was for appearance's sake."

"So, as a nominal Catholic child, what about First Communion and other ceremonial functions?" Chantal continued to ask clarifying questions.

"By the time I was placed with the Rosses, I was almost fifteen. I had essentially aged out of the childhood practices. I think it was simply assumed wherever I had come from, I had satisfied those obligations. After that I more or less skipped through confessions and all."

Richard appeared interested in their conversation but broke in to ask, "What about Andy? First, how did you meet?"

"We met at the University of Edinburgh. Actually, we began to notice each other in the graduate students lounge. Eventually, he asked me out for a pint."

"Both in graduate school?"

"Yes. I was doing my master's and Andy his PhD. I don't consider it a whirlwind romance. We were both very busy with our studies. But we started to spend time together when we could and soon found we got along well and looked forward to seeing each other. Things progressed from there."

"His death must have come as a shock. From what you've said, he sounded like a very active person. He died following a stroke, you said."

"I...I..." Marchesa began to sob.

49

OTTAWA 2011

"I can't do this anymore," Andy said. "What I mean is, maybe I can, but I don't want to."

Marchesa had known this was coming but desperately wanted to argue him...no, not argue, but talk him...out of it. Maybe construct a logical, ethical argument. She knew by the proposed legislation he would not be eligible for assisted dying. Although his physical condition had now deteriorated remarkably, his death was not imminent.

She watched him desperately negotiating his way around their condo in his wheelchair, yet he refused her help. Didn't want to tie her down, he said. Couldn't be talked into an electric wheelchair.

"There's only one electric chair I'd accept. One that would finish the job." He laughed when he noticed her distraught expression. "Oh, Marki," he said. "I don't ever want to leave you. But I want to leave when we can still talk and enjoy each other. I never want to be a vegetable. Just think, me in a vegetative state, and you who tried our whole life together to get me to eat vegetables."

"Andy, don't be so obtuse. You may think you're ready for this, but I'm not...definitely not. Do you want to talk about this now?"

"What?" He laughed. "Vegetables?"

We can't use injectables, she thought. *We don't want tell-tale needle marks raising suspicions. Andy needs to attend the pulmonary fibrosis clinic and appear to be deteriorating but not yet requiring hospitalization or hospice care.* As opposed as she was to Andy's preferences, Marchesa couldn't help think about the logistics. Andy didn't want her to be vulnerable in any way, certainly not for prosecution after his death, yet how could he carry this out without her assistance?

On the days she went into the bioethics office at the hospital, she watched the staffing patterns of the nearby pharmacy department, times of day, shift changes, and personnel involved. For her to wander the hallways would not be considered unusual. It had become well known that she did much of her thinking on her feet and sometimes preferred to walk when she was debating things with herself.

She had her resignation from her part-time consulting position already prepared. *My workload is down. Surely, it won't surprise anyone that I wouldn't want to stay employed after Andy's death.*

She had settled on secobarbital capsules and pentobarbital liquid. Her problem now was acquisition — to avoid having to rush, to avoid making traceable errors. She had come to realize not only her planning, but the ultimate execution of their plan was criminal. *Execution*, she thought. *Ironic.*

She made no notes, did all her research using her work computer, emptying her cache as she went. *I can't remember the dosages. I'll need to search again.*

Andy and I don't want street drugs. We want secure dosages. Proper pharmaceuticals. No agonizing death. Just let Andy slip away. This is driving me crazy. He thinks he has everything settled, his affairs in order. Except for me. I'm not in order.

Andy seemed to be stuck on listening to Anne Murray asking to dance with him or Bryan Adams expressing that he does things for him or maybe for Marchesa.

Marchesa never really kept up with musical artists. Her first experiences with radio were surreptitious searches for news from Allied sources in the Italian prison camp. Then much later in Scotland, she listened to the BBC but still primarily as a news and information source. Once in Montreal, when Andy took up his first position at McGill University, he would find them either French or English language music stations. It was pleasant listening, but it never really registered who the artists were. She didn't make excuses. *I know who Elvis Presley is and who the Beatles are*, she would say when friends would question her lack of knowledge of entertainment personalities. Of course, as an ethicist, she was always wary of celebrity culture as dangerously close to cult behaviour.

Andy certainly knew his trivia. Not just popular music but in so many other topics as well. He even joked that he had accepted his assistant professorship at McGill because it sounded like a Scottish university...McGill.

Andy, please let it go, she thought. *I know you are trying to express your love for me, but I am so unspeakably sad. I guess if it makes him happy. Happy? How can I even think about happy?*

~

It's time! I must do this now! She entered the pharmacy door and walked right up to Pierre, one of the older pharmacists.

"Marchesa," Pierre greeted her with a slight bow. "I still don't have a proper parking spot." Pierre had known her since her early days. He loved to tease her about that original problem she had been faced with at the hospital.

"C'mon Pierre, you take the bus every day."

"Oh, yeah! That! So, what can I do you for today, *madame*?"

"In the department we have been presented with a problem to assess the hospital responsibility in keeping more up to date with drugs, uh…street drugs. Not just for this campus but the whole system. There are so many reports of adulteration of even the deadliest ones like fentanyl. We're worried, as I'm sure you are, that this is way beyond early talk of designer drugs. Everything cut with this, cut with that…"

"Okay."

"David suggested that we need to be more familiar with the legitimate and illegitimate products…is product the right word?'

"Sure, product."

"For street drugs as well?"

Pierre shrugged his shoulders and shook his head. "I guess."

"So, David thought we should be familiar with physical characteristics if we were to comment on them."

"I don't think I understand. If you want street drugs, you use OC Transpo. Have you ever changed buses on Rideau Street—well, actually, at the Rideau Centre? You know that bus stop?"

"That's not my usual route, but what about it?"

"Maybe ask around there. You could come up with all the samples you'd like.'

"Imagine how they'd feel dealing with a septuagenarian, addressing them with research questions."

"A prim and proper one at that." Pierre laughed. "I don't know what I can do for you."

"Maybe if we could look at and handle some of the prescription drugs. Particularly some of the powerful sedative types. I'm at a loss because I don't really know what people look for in a street drug. Maybe we should examine oral presentations, pills, liquids. Maybe barbiturates."

"Okay, maybe something like secobarbital capsules or something with a similar use? I still don't see what you intend to accomplish."

Marchesa shrugged. "I'm not certain I know either."

"Now, for certain, once your group has opened packages and handled preparations, they cannot be put back into use for patient doses. You'll need to return all materials for destruction."

"We would certainly do that."

"In that case, let me check what we have in already opened packages. You wouldn't need something unopened as long as you have a sample package, description, suggested usage, and dosage." He reached to the shelf behind. "You could have this. A bottle of secobarbital, opened and mostly used. Enough capsules left there for you to examine." Pierre continued to scan the shelf, running his finger along the packages. "Here, a package of pentobarbital with two vials left. Would that do?"

It was Marchesa's turn to shrug. "I think so, but what do I know."

"I always thought David was maybe a little off kilter. I'm not going to be mentioning this to Abdul." Pierre was speaking of the chief pharmacist.

Marchesa nodded her agreement.

50

OTTAWA 2011

It was hard for her to believe Andy's life force had left him when he lay in the bed so peacefully. Her thoughts were whirring around in her head. She had insisted he get into bed rather than simply lying on top of it. To avoid raising any suspicions, she'd explained.

As she helped pull the covers over him, she hesitated before she pulled their favourite comforter over him as well. She thought of it as one of the few things they brought from the UK when they emigrated. Embellished with a lovely floral pattern, lightweight and his favourite burgundy colour. They had shopped for it together at Harrod's on one of their London weekends.

Will I ever be able to sleep under it again after this? she thought. *Isn't that just stupid? It's my Andy. I want him to be comfortable.*

Andy swallowed the two drugs easily with a little water to further dilute the pentobarbital. Marchesa held his hand as he lay there. He squeezed her hand gently but otherwise lay quietly. Everything needing to be said had already been shared.

He stopped breathing. Marchesa continued to sit with him. She glanced through the large bedroom window to the balcony, glad that she hadn't closed the blinds. That male cardinal, their male cardinal, had just then, almost at Andy's moment of death, flown in to visit the balcony. Andy had stopped having a bird feeder there, not because he didn't want to feed birds but because the build-up of bird faeces was almost impossible to clean and control. Instead, he had installed a series of mirrors along the rail of the balcony, including a large vertical one at the bedroom end of the terrace, itself inside the railing. Daily, the red male came by to admire himself. Sometimes the female was with him. During the spring mating season and into the summer, the male would sing with exceptional beauty and diversity of song. Uncharacteristically during his usual winter silence, Marchesa was certain that today, he issued his call...*pretty, pretty, pretty*. Real or some kind of chimera, she really didn't know.

Marchesa waited awhile before calling 9-1-1. She continued to sit with Andy for another while. She thought of the time that past June when the male cardinal flew to the large mirror and perched on its frame as usual. But there was another bird with him. She assumed the female, but it seemed to be having trouble trying to find a perch.

"That's an immature male," Andy had said. "Look at the colouring. Just beginning to redden on the chest. See that."

"Yes, okay, I do."

"And the beak is already darkened."

"Ah, yes, he's teaching the youngster about the mirrors...father teaching son!"

"Exactly," Andy had said.

Marchesa sat savouring that memory, looking out at the mirror with only one bird there now. Then she placed the call.

∽

Two police officers arrived first, which surprised Marchesa since she had suggested it was an expected death in a person with pulmonary fibrosis on her 9-1-1 call. The officers were obviously prepared to try to resuscitate Andy but after a quick examination of his lifeless body, the male officer shook his head almost imperceptibly toward his partner, who nodded in agreement almost as indiscernibly. Neither of them attempted CPR.

An ambulance arrived shortly after. Marchesa wondered whether she should have simply called their chosen funeral home for body pickup. However, she did it the way she did to avoid any appearance of impropriety. It had been what she and Andy had agreed.

She answered all the questions put forward by the police and paramedics to what she assumed to be to their satisfaction. She had been careful to bring only two secobarbital capsules and one pentobarbital vial home with her from the office. As soon as she had diluted the pentobarbital, she took the empty vial to dispose of in a neighbourhood dumpster much like was often done in the TV crime series she and Andy watched…disposing of the murder weapon.

∼

Marchesa was surprised two days later to receive a phone call from a detective at the Ottawa Police Service asking if he could come to the condo to ask a few questions. Exactly when, he didn't say.

What do they want? What are they thinking? I answered their questions. Easy, easy, Marchesa thought. *Don't panic. Don't get into a state.*

Just clarification, nothing serious, he'd said. Then Sergeant Duclos came to interview her. As Marchesa recognized it, an interview, hardly a few questions. She was relieved that the body had already been cremated. She realized the police were investigating a possible suicide, a potential overdose of his own pain medication. Did they think she could have helped?

As it was left, there was no suggestion of impropriety, but there was an insinuation that some of the things Andy had said at his most recent fibrosis clinic meeting suggested he could be ready to end his life. Andy, usually circumspect with his remarks, had discussed with some of the others the proposed medically assisted death legislation. So much controversy. Some activist commentators strongly argued the proposed legislation to be inadequate and narrowly defined. Not only that, he thought it so far away from being passed and enacted that it made no sense to wait. That's what he'd shared, and it apparently hinted to what his intentions might actually be.

Although he had been officially retired for eight years, Andy still held an emeritus position and remained well known in the University of Ottawa community. Surprise had been expressed and concern raised about his death when the police interviewed some of his colleagues.

Marchesa was disconcerted that Andy could have expressed his usually private thoughts this way. Thoughts that he had been careful in the past to discuss in confidence with her. *As far as I know*, she thought. *Why now? Or was it his way of saying goodbye?*

Within a few weeks, Marchesa made plans to sell the condo and move away from Ottawa, preferably to Toronto, ill-advised as these types of immediate decisions were often thought to be...

51

TORONTO 2014

As Sandros walked across the baseball field toward the barrier fence below her second-row seats, Marchesa moved down to the front row, to the one seat still sitting empty, anticipating its season ticket holder to arrive for the game.

Sandros peered through the protective netting, bowed slightly, and swept his arm toward her, then laughed. "Aunt Marchesa, good evening. Should I address you as Great-aunt or is simply Aunt okay?"

"It is awkward, isn't it? Aunt is fine. I can't imagine you needing to say Great-aunt every time you talk with me. Actually, realistically, just call me Marchesa. We can be friends as well as relatives."

"Okay then, Marchesa it is!" Sandros paused, then continued, "I have some exciting news for you."

Marchesa quickly thought about whether she'd read anything about any award Sandros might be eligible for. Then she caught her breath. *He's being traded, to Toronto, I hope.*

"Okay, don't keep me in suspense. What news?"

"*Nonna* is coming to Toronto in three weeks."

"To Toronto? Really? I'm...I'm dumbfounded. I don't know what to say."

"Are you pleased?"

"Oh, you don't know how thrilled I am. I stopped myself from dreaming I even had a sister."

"Perhaps I do know. I'm very delighted myself. She does not speak very much English, but she says she is practicing every day. *Nonna* was so excited to talk with you on the telephone."

"I think I'll need to brush up on my Italian."

"*Allora, forse ti aiuterò a fare pratica.*"

"*Grazie.*" Marchesa laughed. "There," she said, "I still have it. But I told Richard and Chantal, she spoke so fast." *That's what I found in Quebec when I heard French spoken*, she thought. *Everyone else talked so fast.*

"We're leaving after the game tonight to play those other Sox and the Nationals. If I was…"

"The other Sox?" Marchesa asked.

"You know, Chicago…the White Sox."

"Yes, yes…the other Sox. Of course."

"That's just what some of us call them. We're the real Sox!"

"Okay, got it!" Marchesa laughed.

Then Sandros continued, "But as I was about to say, if I was still going to be here, we could have talked with *Nonna* again about her travel arrangements."

"I could message her."

Sandros shook his head. "She does not have computer skills or computer literacy. Like many older Italians. Another telephone call would work best. I will call her when I'm home in Boston, but I'll be back here when she flies in."

~

What age would Albertina be now? I think she was seven when we escaped. That's over seventy years ago now. Seventy-seven then. My little sister. Five years younger than me, but I always enjoyed her company. Andy would have liked her. We didn't even talk about her…because she was dead. And now Andy's dead…How I miss him.

Sandros pointed as the door slid open. "There she is," he said excitedly.

Marchesa looked where Sandros pointed but didn't really know who she was looking for. Then a tall, slim woman waved in their direction as she hurried down the ramp with other passengers leaving the customs and immigration area at Toronto Pearson International Airport. She seemed to be struggling with her overly large suitcase.

I used to have that sort of trouble, Marchesa thought. *Then Andy and I got new cases with larger steerable wheels and decent pull handles.*

Sandros rushed forward so he could help his grandmother. "*Nonna, vieni da questa parte per favore. Vi posso aiutare.*"

As he guided his grandmother through the crowds of reuniting families, often five or six individuals there to meet one arriving family member, Italian was spoken freely and filled the air with a buzz. Sandros looked as puzzled as Albertina. They smiled at each other in bewilderment, both for the moment imagining being in Italy, not Toronto.

As they approached her, Marchesa extended both her hands toward her sister, and Albertina reciprocated. Then Marchesa removed her own scarf and gently let it fold around Albertina. "*Ti ricordi che la mamma indossava sempre una sciarpa?*"

Marchesa leaned back to take everything in, looking for familiarity, trying to bridge the almost seventy years since they'd seen each other last.

"*Ciao, sorella mia! Sono Tina!*"

"Oh, my sister! Welcome, Albertina…"

Marchesa enveloped her little sister, Albertina, her lost little sister…Tina…in a warm, lingering hug.

Later, like two excited schoolgirls, they compared how their names defined stages of their lives. Then Albertina insisted emphatically that she was Tina. Albertina was her little girl name.

"But that is how I knew you, how I remember you," Marchesa said.

"*Tina!*" She spoke insistently. "*Ora tocca a Tina!*"

～

In anticipation of her sister's pending arrival, Marchesa had discussed accommodation arrangements with Sandros. When he was here, he lived in a suite at a hotel near the Blue Jays stadium. He said he was prepared for his grandmother to stay with him.

"It is not a stadium view room though," he said, then laughed. "And you know I'm only here for three days before I move on."

"You know she'll sit with me on game days."

"Of course. I was only joking." Sandros laughed again. He seemed as excited as Marchesa that Albertina was coming to Toronto.

"And also, she will stay with me, not in a hotel. My condo has two bedrooms."

"But you don't even know her."

"She is my sister."

"You don't even speak the same language anymore. Even I know what that is like."

Marchesa laughed. "You are totally bilingual ... maybe even multilingual. *Posso parlare abbastanza italiano per parlare con mia sorella.*"

～

"*Questo è così bello,*" Tina said when they walked into the lobby of Marchesa's building. She was wide-eyed.

Marchesa toured Tina and Sandros around the common space available to the residents, including the dining area. Sandros' presence created a stir and quiet murmurs among some of the residents who recognized him.

One of the women called out, "Sandros Audisio! Go Sox go!" Then she and the other women laughed and high-fived each other.

Sandros waved shyly. He was not thinking of being a player right now.

Marchesa took them up the elevator to the seventh floor and into her condo.

"It's a seniors' building," she explained. "We can have medical care if we need it."

Once Sandros translated, Tina looked at Marchesa as if assessing what medical care she could possibly need.

"Oh, not me. *Non me.*"

Tina seemed relieved to realize she was not moving into care for an invalid. Earlier discussion as they left the taxi in front of the building had left her confused, Marchesa describing one half of the building as residential and the other half as a nursing home.

52

Once the Red Sox series was finished and Sandros and the team had left town, Marchesa had not taken Tina to the short two game series against the Detroit Tigers. Instead, they watched most of each game on TV.

Today, however, with the Jays having also left town for a series in Houston, she determined this was the day when Tina should start to experience how she lived in Toronto, her day-to-day activities, her city. She decided it would be easier to take a cab to My Spot, explaining in a careful mixture of English and Italian that they would walk home later.

I think I got that across, she thought. *Isn't English wonderful? As a language, almost anything goes.* Marchesa reflected on her first experiences when Drago insisted that they would speak only English. It did not take long before she had achieved reasonable fluency.

She explained to Tina that she wanted to take her to meet friends of hers who came to this *ristorante, questa caffetteria* most mornings each week. Tina understood the coffee shop concept. Marchesa knew she would because of her own childhood memories of a local *caffè* in Bergamo where their father, the mayor, was a welcome customer, even during the initial stages of the war.

She also explained that this evening, they would watch the Blue Jays-Astros game on TV. She hoped to give Tina a better understanding of the game before they attended another live match and take advantage of the opportunity when she wasn't focussed solely on her grandson. Marchesa thought she was being careful not to pack too much into a day. She noticed Tina seemed to tire easily, but she didn't know how to interpret that. She hoped Tina simply hadn't recovered from her jet lag yet. She also knew watching and spending time with Sandros could be exhausting in itself.

They left Queen Victoria Gardens about the same time as they would if they had been walking. Marchesa didn't know how long they might need to wait for a cab. But there was one, as if anticipating them, in the taxi space across the street. Consequently, they were at My Spot ahead of the regulars. That gave some time to get seated and talk with Ben.

Marchesa was pleased to see Sally was there, getting ready to serve customers. She introduced them to Tina. "Ben, Sally, I would like you to meet my sister, Tina, who has come to visit all the way from Italy."

"Welcome Tina," Ben said. "*Benvenuta.*"

"Oh, Marsha, it is such a pleasure to meet your sister," Sally said.

Tina frowned briefly and almost cringed in shyness like the little sister of so long ago. She seemed appreciative of the welcome she received but was obviously puzzled hearing her sister addressed as Marsha.

Marchesa whispered to Tina, indicating with her hands that it was all right.

In a few minutes, Sally brought two of Marchesa's favourite double espressos. Tina sipped hers almost immediately even though it was very hot. "*Questo è un buon caffè.*"

When Sally looked over to the table, Tina caught her eye with a slight wave and nodded her affirmative approval.

Around eight o'clock, some of the others who shared Marchesa's table arrived. Marchesa made introductions, all the while hoping she would remember everyone's name. Introducing people was not within her comfort zone. Andy always came through in those situations.

Formalities finished, everyone went back to their usual conversations. Marchesa watched for Richard and Chantal, hoping they would show up today. She so wanted Tina to spend a little more time with Chantal. She wasn't sure why, but she simply had a feeling they would be simpatico.

53

"You could come down to Boston when the Blue Jays come to play us," Sandros said on the phone. He was quite diligent in phoning since the Red Sox left Toronto. He seemed to realize his *Nonna* would appreciate more family support than Marchesa might be able to offer on her own.

He knew that Marchesa was working hard to speak Italian. He knew from his own experience how quickly one was able to regain a childhood language. He also recognized Marchesa to be a person who would be embarrassed to be out-of-date.

He continued to express his thoughts. "Maybe you could even look around for a place to share with *Nonna* in Boston."

"No," Marchesa said. "Toronto is my home. I like it here. This is where Andy wished to spend his retirement years. I'm here for Andy. And don't you think your *Nonna* will go back to Italy before long?"

"I don't know," Sandros said. "I haven't asked her about her intentions."

"Nor have I. Wouldn't that be a good starting point before we assume too much?"

"You are right about that." He laughed good-naturedly. "You said you're living in Toronto for Andy. You haven't told me very much about Andy."

"Andy and I were together almost fifty-six years." She hesitated before continuing. "I...I want to feel he is still with me."

"Maybe next time I'm in Toronto, we could talk a bit about him."

"Okay, we'll do that for certain. In the meantime..." Marchesa laughed. "To accommodate *Nonna* and me, couldn't you request a trade to the Jays?"

"Wait a minute. Where did that come from? I like playing for the Red Sox! Put *Nonna* on the phone. Maybe I could talk with her and get away from all your pressure. Or is she scheming along with you?"

Marchesa laughed along with Sandros. "But seriously now," she said, "I've been talking with an immigration lawyer. She thinks, since I'm a Canadian citizen, I should have no trouble sponsoring Tina to come live with me in Toronto."

"Really?" Sandros was surprised because he'd never considered Marchesa would have acted so quickly. "That would be fantastic!"

54

"You know, Marsha...Marchesa," said Richard. "You have quite a life story that you've shared with Chantal and me. I think, and I'm sure Chantal agrees, your story is very intriguing, somewhat mysterious from a Jays fan point of view and definitely worth sharing as a biography."

"But...it is too personal. I've never shared as much as I have with you two. Except with Andy, of course. I'm not comfortable with you telling my story. And I can't even imagine who would be interested."

Richard glanced toward Chantal and nodded his head. She took over. "We think the three of us...you, me and Richard...should author this biography, or really, autobiography."

"But...what makes me so important to warrant publishing my story?"

"Here's the reality. You are seen on television during every Blue Jays home game," Chantal said with excitement. "That's how we first saw you and became interested in talking with you. There would be all sorts of Jays fans who would love to read your story. I even remember looking at the screen, noticing you were never dressed in anything remotely Blue Jays. No memorabilia. Nothing related to baseball. But you were always so nicely dressed and always with a beautiful scarf. I thought at the time that I'd really love to see that women's scarf closet. There's a lot of buzz out there and speculation about who you are. You are my story."

Marchesa laughed.

Richard picked up the discussion. "Now that Sandros and Tina have entered the picture, your story is even more fascinating."

"I've never seen myself as particularly interesting. All through our married life Andy, was the person people wanted to talk to. And talk about. Now the others in my seat section, and at the coffee shop too, want to ask me about Sandros."

"Yes, you have a series of interesting characters in your history," Richard said. "That starts with your parents and the reasons you were imprisoned as a family. Imagine, thrown into a prisoner-of-war camp by your own country! And we're just getting started there."

"Okay, I see what you're saying, Richard. But didn't these things happen to many others also?"

Chantal said, "I can't even imagine the almost two years you spent trekking across Europe with Drago as your guide, and your good fortune in landing with a family in Scotland."

"So much of that was luck, blind luck. Then I met Andy and landed in Canada. What absolute luck!"

"Maybe, but then me being here is just good fortune also!" Richard said.

"I see what you're saying, Richard. What do you think, Chantal?"

"Oh, don't worry, I see my own life as more than fortunate, to the side of privileged. Growing up in a skiing family. Progressing to a career in sports and now writing about sports. And, as an added bonus, because of you, Richard and I are getting together."

"Wait, did you just try to slip that by me as part of your argument. You're really getting together?"

"Yes, we are!"

"Wow! That makes me happy! I foresaw you would be suited to each other long ago."

"Thank you. We're very excited. We're already looking at condo properties. But, back to the discussion before we get too far off track. You are intellectual, educated. You went to graduate school.

You chose a career in ethics to make sure other people would be treated properly, with dignity."

"What Chantal said before…We think it should be the three of us who tell the story, write the story, co-author the story," Richard said.

"I'm not convinced. Although, believe me, you are starting to intrigue me." Then her thoughts devolved to her Andy, to her part in his death, and she was terrified. Her terror was always just below the surface. It was her life. His death. Could she minimize or remove it from her consciousness to tell her story?

"You said you already have a title in mind?" Marchesa continued. "I mean, you're both so far ahead of me on this."

"We were thinking *Home Plate Lady*." Chantal seemed so pleased and excited with her revelation.

"That's not how I see myself, and I would have trouble being portrayed that way. You know how I feel about labelling someone. And I always insist on referring to the gender as woman, not lady. Lady presumes some sort of social status. Often, it's used as a pejorative. The person using it doesn't always think the woman worthy of the implied compliment. But lady isn't nearly as bad as *girl*. There I go, not answering the question at hand but off into an ethical analysis."

"That's okay, but how about something like *Home Plate Woman*?"

"No, that really doesn't have much of a ring to it, does it? Look at me just jumping on board with you two." Marchesa paused. "I'm imagining something more along the line of *Woman Behind Home Plate*." She paused again. "Let me think about it."